SENTENCED

A Little Pile of Stories

Nina Herbst

CONTENTS

Title Page
The Most Silent Night   1
Magic In the Morning   5
Blood in the Temple   10
The Gingerbread Man   20
The Surprise Party   25
Pinky Promise   30
Becoming Invisible   34
Resigned   40
No Stars For You   44
Crazy Cate   48
Mirror|Mirror   54
Target(ed)   56
MidTerm Exam   60
Teacher of the Year   64
The Guide   69
Ghostly Characterizations   73
Haunting 101   78
Death Wish   82
Uncovered   87
Diary Dearest   93

Missing Cat: Reward if Found	96
Pinder	100
Lily	104
The Mailbox	107
Burning Bridges	111
The Professor's Secret	128
Locked	133
Self(ie) Portrait	138
The Black Box	143
Touched	148
Book Club Questions to Ponder over Pinot	154

(Anticipated) Praise for "Sentenced":
"This book changed my life!"
- You (you just don't know it yet)

"The stories warmed my heart."
- Probably my mom.

"This book was perfect for killing time while I waited in the parking lot for my kid to finish practice. I'd just read a few stories and time would fly by!"
- All the sports moms transporting kids to games and practices

"We chose this for our Book Club, and had so much to talk about when we met!"
- Lying Book Club member (we all know they just have drinks and snacks and don't really talk about the book.)

Also Written by Nina Herbst:
Shopping lists
Post It Notes (so many Post It Notes…)
(Unfinished) To-Do Lists
Lost Poetry (where did I put that notebook?)
Lunch Box jokes

Questions, comments, and invitations to Book Club meetings and/or cat birthday parties can be sent to NinaHerbst98@aol.com

One Christmas, not too long ago, we almost lost my dad. As I sat waiting up through the night to hear if his surgery was a success, I thought about how I'd always wanted to put together stories for him. For as long as I can remember, he'd always tell me "write that down."

He made it, I started writing. Then stopped, stumped. Then stumbled upon a site giving story prompts. The majority of the stories collected here are a result of those prompts, which explains why the content runs the gamut of humans, holidays, pets, and aliens. Tomorrow is never promised, so here we are.

For Mom and Dad, who are always there for me

The following stories are fiction. Unless otherwise indicated, all the names, places, characters, businesses, and incidents are either the product of the author's imagination or used in a fictitious manner. Any resemblance to actual persons or events, living or dead, is coincidental. Some may be based on actual events, yet changed for dramatic purposes as creative non-fiction.

Sentenced: A Little Pile of Stories. Copyright 2023 by Nina Herbst. All Rights reserved. No part of this book may be used or reproduced in any manner whatsoever without written permission, except in the case of brief quotations embodied in critical articles and reviews.

THE MOST SILENT NIGHT

Holly wreaths and red bows swam around in a blurry sea in front of me. I sniffled as a stray tear dropped onto the wrapping paper I had just taped down. I put the gift aside and looked around the room for another to wrap. I could hear the faint sound of my mom's television in the next room. Late night television held limited options, but I'm pretty sure she wasn't paying much attention to it anyway. It was 2:03am. Christmas Eve. About six hours since Dad went into the operating room. We hadn't yet told my sister, out of town with her in-laws. What could she do anyway but worry? She knew he wasn't feeling well this week, but didn't know it came to this.

A trip to the ER, and emergency surgery.

I heard the sound of feet shuffling down the wooden floor of the hallway. My mom peeked her head in the room.

"Almost done?"

I know she meant wrapping the Santa gifts for the kids, but I think she also meant the surgery. Why hadn't they called yet? It shouldn't take this long.

"Yep. Just a few more." I said with a forced smile.

"Do you think they'll call soon? It's so late. Why is it taking this long?" My mom said as she absently put her hands in her robe pockets.

"I'm sure everything is fine. They said it was complicated, so it's probably just taking longer than expected. They'll call soon."

"I'm sure you're right," my mom softly said as she made her way back to her room.

I sat on the bed in my parent's spare room, and glanced out the window into the darkness. I thought back to Christmases growing up, in a different house and different time.

***

Chocolate chip cookies. That's what sat heavy in my belly as I lay on my back, head under the Christmas tree as it slowly turned around. I was 9, and had spent many an evening like that growing up. Watching the lights move past like shooting stars in slow motion from under the tree. The tree stand had a little motor and each year, our tree spun dizzily in the living room. There was a Christmas record playing in the dining room, and I whisper-sang along to Kenny Rogers and Dolly Parton dueting "A Christmas to Remember". I had folded a teeny piece of paper and lodged it next to the power button to keep it on, otherwise it wouldn't stay pressed in. A trick my dad thought of. Back then, we didn't buy new things if something went wrong; my dad always found a way to fix them, even if temporarily.

He had been working that day, came home, and was off again somewhere. Maybe the grocery store? Mom was cleaning in the kitchen, then went upstairs to put away laundry. My sister was on the phone in her room.

I rolled over to my side and looked at the Nativity that sat under the tree. I traced at the rough brown mossy pieces glued to the sloping roof with my fingers. Jesus didn't look like a baby in our Nativity, but a tiny adult with outstretched hands in a little plastic straw bed. Sort of unsettling. Mary's paint was imprecise and the blue from her dress washed into her face and cheeks. Joseph was surprisingly presentable.

Christmas was coming, and a warm excitement filled me like strings of colorful lights wrapped around my veins all throughout my body. It was my absolute favorite time of year. Christmas Eve would mean dinner at my Grandmother's house. The smell of various fishes cooked various ways heavy in the air like a seafood fog. And my favorite, the mushrooms. I have no idea how my uncle made them, but I looked forward to them each year. I tried to replicate them a few times, failing each. Mushrooms and soy sauce? Wine? It took a magic to make those mushrooms, and I never quite figured out the spell.

Then a noise outside had gotten my attention and I rolled out from under the tree. I looked out the large bay window in the front of my house and saw my dad's car pulled into the driveway. He was home from wherever he'd been. I slid onto the couch and grabbed my book from the table.

I had just turned the page when the front door opened. I looked up and saw my dad walking into the foyer, a huge smile on his face. A smile that said he'd been up to something.

"Hey dad!" I said and put my book aside. He was walking in slowly, looking around, and holding his coat. This was an odd entrance.

"Hey sweetheart!" He said as he decided to come into the living room.

He didn't sit down, just stood there smiling, fidgeting with his coat. Then I thought I heard a soft sound from somewhere. What was that? I heard it again. A high pitched cry like a baby cooing. I looked at my dad, puzzled.

Then he opened his coat slowly, and from inside the pocket he pulled out the smallest fluffy ball of mewing fur.

"A kitten! You have a kitten!" I squealed.

"Shh! I didn't tell your mother!" he replied, glancing over his shoulder to see if my mom heard and was coming.

"You have a *secret* kitten! What's her name? I love her! Is it a girl? It looks like a girl!" I said and took the warm fluff into my arms. She mewed again as I snuggled my face into her brown and black fur. She was the tiniest kitten I'd ever seen.

"Yes, she's a girl. And she's a runt. Smallest kitten in her litter. When I saw her I knew she had to come home with me. Nearly tore apart my car on the way here! She's a feisty runt!" he said.

"She's just perfect! I love her," I said as she squirmed out of my arms and darted like a mini cheetah over to the front window. She looked back at us, looking at her, and leaped into the sheer white curtains that adorned the window. She used her claws to scale all the way to the top, then sat on the curtain rod inches from the ceiling, looking down on us with beautiful mischievous yellow eyes.

My dad and I looked at each other and laughed.

"What should we call her?" he asked.

"Since it's almost Christmas, let's call her Holly."

And then Holly swung over the curtain rod, dug in her claws, and slid down the curtain shredding it as she descended to the floor. I gasped. Dad laughed. Holly ran.

"Holly Claws!" My dad laughed and showed me his arms, scratched up from his ride home with her.

I looked at the shredded curtains and thought about the look my mom's face would have when she saw the destruction and the secret kitten. As I smiled at the thought and the curtains, something caught my eye in the window. Snow. It had just started to snow. A soft, quiet, slowly falling snow.

My heart was full, happy, content.

***

I was brought back to my parent's spare room with the sound of my mom's cell ringing. I heard her answer, saying "Hello? Yes, this is she…"

It must be the hospital. I looked at my phone. It was 6:08am. I still hadn't slept. Neither of us had. I wondered what this call would mean for this Christmas. They say miracles can happen at Christmas. I squeezed my eyes closed, trying to hear my mom's conversation, but it was silent.

I opened my eyes, and looked to the window. It had just started to snow. A soft, quiet, slowly falling snow.

My heart was full, happy, content. I smiled. And I knew.

MAGIC IN THE MORNING

Frannie lay still as a fence post snuggled in bed, her little sister pressed up beside her. She had been up for hours, staring out her bedroom window into the darkness, only the white twinkling of stars dotting the night sky. Soon, it would be morning. Frannie's tummy gave an excited tumble, as she thought of the presents that surely awaited her and CeCe under the tree.

She smiled, and gently stroked her sister's soft blonde curls. Her sleeping sounds were quiet and rhythmic, her chest rising and falling and keeping time. She smelled like cookies and cinnamon. Frannie pressed her face close to her sister and breathed in, thinking of how excited she was the night before.

"I don't even think I'll be able to sleep tonight, Frannie!"

"Me too, CeCe! What do you think Santa will bring you?"

"I just know he will bring me a doll with curls just like mine! And she will have a bottle and a bib, and I'll put her to sleep in the crib Poppa made me!"

"That sounds wonderful CeCe! Know what I hope I'll get? New paper, paint, and paintbrushes. I've been out of them for months now. I hope I get new painting things!" Frannie said, squeezing her hands together.

"I hope so too, Frannie! You paint the most beautiful pictures I've ever seen." CeCe answered, a look of admiration washing over her small face.

Frannie knew her parents didn't have much to spend on them for Christmas. Her father spent every day, from dawn to dusk, working in the coal mines. Except Sunday. That was their family day. Her mother worked in the textile factory, and Frannie stayed home to take care of CeCe. She knew it wouldn't be long until she would go with her mother to the factory though. Then CeCe would go to their neighbor's til they got home. But then there would be more money.

"Do you want to leave out a cookie and milk for Santa? And a carrot for his reindeer?" Frannie asked CeCe, who had wandered to the window looking for their father to get home.

"Yes! Let's leave it out now so we don't forget!" CeCe replied and ran to get a plate and glass.

The girls left the cookie and milk near the fireplace, just as their father walked through the door.

"Poppa! You're home! And guess what! Santa is coming tonight!" CeCe yelled, and threw her tiny arms around her soot covered father, dirty from the mines.

"That's right, darlin', he sure is! But he only comes if you've been a good girl. Hmm, have you and Frannie been good this year?"

"Yes, Poppa!" the girls said in unison.

Their parents smiled and exchanged a look that seemed to say they agreed.

"Then just maybe when you wake up tomorrow, Santa will have left you two something. Now, what's there to eat tonight? I'm hungrier than a deer in the winter!" Poppa said as he took off his hat and gloves.

"Momma's made a special dinner, you know that! We have it every Christmas Eve!" Frannie laughed.

"Oh, she did? Well, what do you know! She did! I'll get cleaned up, then we will all sit down and eat!" Poppa said.

"Help me set the table, girls. Your father may start eating the chair soon if we don't put the food out!" Momma said giggling.

Frannie thought of their wonderful Christmas Eve dinner, followed by singing Christmas Carols by the tree. Her favorite was "The First Noel", but she loved so many of them it was hard to choose just one favorite. Frannie sat by Momma, leaning into her strong arms that held her tight. CeCe was nestled like a baby bird on Poppa's lap by the warm, radiant fire. Finally, the girls sleepily climbed the worn wooden ladder to their bed loft, and had tried to go to sleep.

Now, after laying awake for what seemed like an eternity to Frannie, she decided to slip out of bed and take a peek down by the tree. She so wished for her painting things, she just had to see if they were there.

Slowly, carefully, she inched away from her slumbering sister. She stretched her bare feet to the cold wooden floor beside their bed. She knew just where the creaky boards were, and carefully tiptoed around each one.

Downstairs, Momma and Poppa were also unable to sleep. They quietly opened the cedar chest at the foot of their bed, blindly reaching inside. Underneath spare blankets and summer clothes that were neatly folded and put away, Momma felt the first package. Her fingers felt the rough red string that was tied around the brown paper. CeCe's doll. She cautiously pulled it out, careful not to tear the paper. Next, she found another small present, similarly wrapped, and pulled that one out too. CeCe's bottle for her new baby doll. She felt a tingle run through her. CeCe will be so excited to open exactly what she had wished for this Christmas. She placed the presents on the floor next to the chest, and reached in on the other side. She felt the package she had wrapped for Frannie. A larger one than CeCe's but painting supplies and paper made for a bigger present. She pulled it from the chest, and gleamed at the green ribbon holding everything together. Frannie could get lost for hours in her paintings. Landscapes, animals, people. She even made their rickety, falling down barn look surreal in a painting. Momma knew Frannie would love all her new supplies. Work had been kind this year, and Momma and Poppa saved enough to put aside to get their girls what they wanted for Christmas. Which made it a wonderful Christmas for all of them.

Poppa came close to Momma and whispered, "There's one more package in there. Keep looking," with an expectant grin, hoping she'd like what he secretly saved for to surprise her.

"What's this?" Momma whispered as she felt another package amongst the linens.

"Open it!"

Momma carefully opened the small package that fit neatly in her hand. She tried to stifle her excitement, but she let out the smallest gasp before clapping her hand to mouth.

"It's beautiful!" she whispered, immediately placing the delicate gold chain around her neck. Hanging from the chain, a small gold cross rested gently on her white nightgown. It was just like the one her Gram had worn.

"Merry Christmas, darlin'," Poppa said, as Momma hugged him tight.

"Now, let's get these presents out there before the littlins' wake up!"

Frannie hadn't heard a thing as she crossed her bedroom floor and came to the ladder overlooking the main floor of the small cabin. She bent down, and crawled the rest of the way to see over.

Momma and Poppa were at the tree. They had just placed the gifts down, and started to head back to their bedroom on the other side of the fireplace.

Frannie looked to the tree, and something caught her eye. A small white flash of something, something that seemed to move quickly then disappear toward her parent's room.

Momma hurried Poppa ahead of her, sneaking out of sight and grabbing her long white nightgown and pulling it quickly close, right as she heard a rustling above. Momma and Poppa stood still as a fence post as they waited for Frannie to get back in bed. Had she seen them? Did she know? They looked at each other, waiting. Momma felt a knot in her stomach. They were always so careful on Christmas Eve, and now?

"Santa!" Frannie whispered.

"CeCe! Wake up! Wake up! Santa was here! And guess what! I SAW his magic sweep him up and away through the chimney! It was a white flash, and he disappeared! And there are presents!" Frannie tried to whisper, not quite succeeding. Momma breathed, finally.

"Santa came?" CeCe rubbed her eyes and tried to understand what was happening. It was not yet morning, still dark, but it was...Christmas! She sat up and hugged Frannie.

"Merry Christmas, Frannie!"

"Merry Christmas, CeCe! We have to wait here though til the sun comes up. You know the Christmas Rule. No going down til the sun is up!" Frannie reminded her excited sister.

"I know, I'm just so excited! Did it look like my gift was a baby doll? Did it? Even if it's not, that's ok, but I really want a baby doll!"

"I couldn't tell. But I think it is! Snuggle up close to stay warm and we'll watch the window til the sun lights up the sky! Then we can go down!"

Frannie hugged CeCe close, and imagined all the paintings she was going to create. He came!

Momma hugged Poppa close, and imagined another Christmas morning with the magic of Santa for her little girls.

BLOOD IN THE TEMPLE

I'm not Jewish, but blood collectors don't care who you worship when they set up drives for a blood harvest. Every year on Christmas Eve, my sister and I would travel down the long avenue in our town until the bright glowing menorah was in view. We'd pull in, get in line, and fill out the obligatory paperwork. Are you feeling ill today? Have you been out of the country? Is your blood tainted by germs or foreign lands?

This year was no different. We had Christmas music playing, and very soon pulled in and parked, ready to begin our blood-letting tradition.

We hung our winter coats in the closet in the lobby, and walked right up to take our places in line.

Once we muddled through the papers, it was time for the finger prick to see if our blood had what it takes to move forward in the process. I watched the nurse stab my finger and aggressively squeeze out its red liquid, barely falling short of squeezing my nail from my finger as well into the vial.

Then we watched to see if it had enough iron to weigh it down to the bottom of the vial. Go go go little droplet!, I cheered in my head. Once it hit the bottom I smiled and squeaked "yes!" under my breath. I made it to the next round!

I was called over to a pop-up donation table and sat obediently as the nurse tied a rubber strip around my arm.

"Excited for Christmas?" She unenthusiastically queried.

"Yeah of course! How about you?" I replied.

"I guess. I have to work so hopefully it goes by fast," she glumly told me.

I felt for the healthcare workers who often had holidays in hospitals. I gave her a sympathetic smile and nod to try to tell her I hoped so too.

She told me to lay back, so I glanced behind me hoping I'd

land on the little plastic pillow awaiting my head. With a flick of a needle and a pull of a tube, my blood began flowing from the tender crease opposite my bony elbow. I felt the warmth of it as it made its way through the plastic tube, down over my arm, and into a bag positioned below the table.

"Ok, just relax now and I'll be back to check on you," Nurse Glumly (as I named her in my head) told me before walking away.

"Thank you!" I chirped, as I tried not to think about the blood exiting me towards the Temple floor. I had been sure to eat something before I came, but I always seemed to feel nauseous when giving blood. Was it from the blood loss or just the "thought" of blood loss? I wasn't sure.

I looked around the mildly crowded room and spotted my sister laying on a table, her bag nearly filled already.

Overachiever.

I watched as smiling nurses came over and nodded approvingly at her hefty red plastic bag, bulging with blood. They happily untethered her arm, applied a bandaid, and had her sit up for a few minutes before she made her way to the snack table for juice and Christmas cookies. Or would they have Hanukkah cookies here? Is that even a thing? I wondered that as she walked to the table and caught my eye, smiling and giving me a thumbs up. And, was that the Rocky theme music playing in the background as she strode away?

She looked down at my bag and her smile turned into a puzzled look before she tried to smile again. Why would she look at my bag like that? If there's one thing my sister can't do, it's hide her facial expressions. I knew something was off. Just as I tried to figure out what that could be, Nurse Glumly walked back over, frowning at my bag. She gave the tube a little shake as if to encourage the reluctant blood to make its way down the tube. She handed me a little ball with a smiley face that had been worn away from years of squeezing. The happy squeezy ball had just one eye left and half a smile.

"Squeeze this ball and let's try to get some more blood

flowing," she said before walking to the man at the next table.

I followed her instructions and squeezed Mr. Smiley tight to make the blood flow faster. The sooner this could be over the better. We had Christmas Eve dinner soon at my grandmother's house. I glanced over at my sister who was having juice and Hanukkah cookies (I've decided it IS a thing).

I made it a challenge to try to squeeze out as much as possible and fill that bag whether my veins wanted to cooperate or not. I heard an imaginary crowd cheering me on, chanting "Fill that bag! Fill that bag!"

I couldn't see my progress because of my prone posture, but I was certain a full bag victory would be mine! I imagined it growing like the Grinch's heart. My bag will grow three sizes this day! I began to feel a bit lightheaded, no doubt due to my excitement at winning the Bag Race.

As if to substantiate my thoughts, I saw Nurse Glumly look at her watch then look at my paperwork in her hands. She must see I'm done, having reached the finish line and ready to be pinched off.

Nurse Glumly walked over and with a sigh, said "Well, you're all done."

I smiled as she swiftly swiped the needle lodged in my arm. My smile faded when I saw her lift my bag, which looked like a half-finished Capri Sun that a toddler discarded.

What happened? Why didn't it fill after squeezing and willing my blood out?

"Oh don't worry. We can send it out to be used in lab testing since you went over the 15 minute collection time and only partially filled the bag," Nurse Glumly dryly said as she packed up the bag and tubes.

Lab testing? Was she serious?

Nurse Glumly caught the look of surprise and disappointment on my face and tried to offer some consolation.

"If you see a clone of yourself in a few years you'll know what they used your blood for," she said and smiled ever so slightly for the first time tonight.

Defeated, I sat slowly up and thought about a second ME walking the streets all because I couldn't squeeze Mr. Smiley hard enough and get my blood out. Would she be better at math than me? Probably not. I walked to the snack table, but didn't feel like a Hanukkah cookie.

"Here. Eat this. You're looking a little pale and clammy," my sister said as she slid a cookie over like an air hockey puck.

"I'm fine, really. But I don't think they can use my blood for anyone. It wasn't fast enough," I said, failing to hide my disappointment.

"Yeah, I heard. That's ok, they can still use it for something. And lab work is important too," she tried to reassure me. But didn't.

"You're right. It's fine. Maybe next time."

I faked a smile and looked at the cookie in front of me. As I stared at it, it seemed to get blurry. I squeezed my eyes closed, then opened them again to focus. Hmm. Now that was odd. The chatter in the room became a low humming sound and I could feel my face getting hot. Then, the noise disappeared and my face wasn't hot anymore. Maybe I should have eaten more before donating today. I felt my stomach get queasy again, then all of a sudden it went away and I felt fine again.

Relieved, I decided to try some juice and looked around for the girl helping out and bringing the snacks to the table. Instead, I spotted a very young girl walking in, alone. I looked behind her, but didn't see anyone, and wondered what she could be doing there. Maybe just on the prowl for some juice and cookies? She was smiling and cradled an old-fashioned Cabbage Patch Kid doll. It struck me that it was the exact doll I had when I was her age. Yellow loops of yarn made her a curly-haired cherub of a doll, with a pink dress and lace trim on the hem and sleeves.

Still not seeing an adult to claim her, I walked over to her.

"Hi! Are you with your parents here? Can I help you find them or maybe you just wanted a snack?" I asked.

"Oh, hi! I've been looking for you!" she said with an innocent grin.

Looking for me? What?

"You were looking for me?" I asked her, clearly puzzled.

"Yes! You're to come with me. I'd like to show you something. And, do you remember this doll?" she asked.

"Of course, I had one just like it when I was your age. Same hair, dress, everything. Why?" I asked, wondering where this was going.

"Do you remember when you got your doll?"

"It was from Santa, for Christmas," I recalled.

She smiled and pointed to a TV on the wall in the next room. There was a show on, but I didn't recognize it.

"Look," she said.

I squinted my eyes and began to walk closer. There was a scene playing out on the TV. A little girl, laying on the floor, crying. She was staring at a brand new box holding a Cabbage Patch Doll. There were rolls of wrapping paper next to her.

"That's...me." I said in disbelief. What was going on? Why am I watching myself as a little girl crying over a toy?

"I remember that," I whispered as I watched. "It was my friend's birthday, and we were giving her a Cabbage Patch Kid doll. I wanted one so very badly. I was so upset she was getting one and I didn't have one," I softly said. Could anyone else see this? I looked around but nobody was paying attention to us.

"Do you remember what your mother said as you cried on the floor?" the little girl asked, her eyes big blue wells of knowing.

"She said it was better to give than to receive."

I remembered so vividly those words. And just as I thought about it, there was my mother on the screen saying them. Child-me looked up and nodded at my mother, but I knew it didn't make the disappointment go away.

"I was sad I wasn't getting a Cabbage Patch Kid. Then, when I got one at Christmas, I thought maybe it was ok not to have the things we want WHEN we want them. There's comfort in knowing you may get that thing someday. And I thought about that other times in my life when I didn't get what I wanted. I just had to be patient and maybe I'd get it someday," I explained. But it seemed the little girl already knew what I was thinking before I said it.

Just then, the TV went dark. I looked beside me, and the little girl with the Cabbage Patch Doll wasn't there anymore. I looked around the room, but didn't see a trace of her.

"Looking for someone?" a teenage boy said from behind me.

Startled, I turned quickly and saw a boy who looked vaguely familiar, but I couldn't place him. His brown eyes and dark curly hair drew me in, and I felt like I wanted nothing more than to talk to him.

"Yes, I mean, no, I was just...did you see a little girl walk away from here?" I asked hopefully.

"Nope. No little girls at the Temple now. But why are YOU at the Temple now? Shouldn't you be out with your friends or working or something?" he asked.

"It's Christmas Eve. I don't have work today and my friends are doing family things. Which I will also be doing very soon."

And I thought for a moment about how much time lately I've been out with friends or working max hours at the local grocery store after school and on weekends. My sister had asked me to have lunch with her and my mom the other day, and I declined yet again. I couldn't even remember the last time I put aside plans with friends or work to hang out with my sister and parents. We used to have dinner out once a week and talk about life, tell stories, and laugh. When did that slip away?

"You are pretty lucky to have a family who wants to spend time together, you know. Not everyone has that," he said with a serious look. He had warm, gentle eyes, and a smile that seemed connected to his heart.

"You're right. I think I've been spending less time than I should with mine," I said with downcast eyes. I looked over at my sister chatting with other donors at the table. I was glad we had a long break from school ahead of us. I thought about her graduation coming up this June, and how she'd be going away to college. I should have been seizing those opportunities to hang out with her and my parents more often.

"That's my sister over there. We come here together each year to give blood. She's much better at it than me though, apparently. Like science and math…" I cracked a smile thinking of how alike yet different we were. She's on time, I'm last minute. She likes math, I like art.

I looked up and thought about how lucky I was to have a sister and family to spend Christmas with. I opened my mouth to say as much to the boy with the dark curly hair, but he wasn't there. Gone, like the little girl.

A little unsettled, I walked back to the table and sat down again at the only open seat left. I was ready to leave. I was ready to rethink things in my life. I'd been pretty self-centered lately, and needed to think of others too. I needed to really treasure what I had.

The man next to me nudged my arm. He was quite old, his paper thin skin barely hanging on to his bony face. His eyes were hollow and dark. I couldn't tell if his eyes were brown or black, sunken into his face. He nudged again and pointed across the room at Nurse Glumly. I should probably find out her real name, I thought to myself.

"The nurse? Do you know her?" I asked.

The man slowly nodded his head. He was dressed in all black, from head to toe. He carried a cane, resting at his legs, with a marble skull on the top of it.

"She seems kinda sad, doesn't she," I remarked.

The man in black slowly nodded again.

"I'm not sure if she has any plans for Christmas. She didn't say much. But, I guess I didn't ask much either," I said, regretfully.

He looked at me with his hollow eyes, then back at her as he took his cane and slowly walked across the room to the corner. He appeared to be waiting for something. He pulled a gold pocket watch from his coat pocket, gave the faintest grin, then stood again tapping the skull on his cane.

I looked from him to Nurse Glumly, back to him. Something didn't feel right.

Something felt very wrong.

Something felt like it was churning in my belly, and heating my face, humming in my ears, and burning my eyes.

I became aware of bright lights around me, and heard my sister's voice.

"I think she's coming around now!" My sister said to someone I couldn't see.

I blinked my eyes and rubbed them. I was in a small room, not at the table anymore.

"What happened? Where am I?" I managed to say.

"You were sitting at the table by me, one minute eating a cookie and the next you were flat on the floor. We moved you into this room out of the way."

Trying to piece together what happened, I looked around for the little girl, and the curly haired boy. Then I quickly looked to the corner for the man in black. Nothing. They weren't there.

"I feel ok. I think I can walk," I said as I put a hand on my head, and felt sick to my stomach.

"You wait here a minute. I'm going to go to the lot and start my car to warm it up a little before you get in. Just sit and relax, ok?" my sister ordered.

"Ok, I'll be fine. I'll wait here."

My sister walked out to get her car heated up, and I sat trying to figure out what happened.

Nurse Glumly came in and sat by me.

"Gave us a scare when you fell down. How's your head? You really hit it," she said, with a worried look on her face.

"It still hurts. I guess I passed out, huh?" I asked, knowing the answer.

"It's ok. Lots of people do. You'll start feeling better soon. You won't even be late for your family dinner," She said with a forced smile.

"What about you? Headed to a family dinner tonight?" I

intruded.

"No, not for me. I don't have kids, I'm getting divorced right now, and my parents passed away earlier this year. I guess that just leaves cereal or leftovers when I get home," she tried to joke.

"Come to our dinner then. There's always way too much food, my aunt makes the best Yule Log dessert and if we're lucky, she went easy on the rum icing this year. Say yes. I owe you for saving my life tonight," I pleaded.

"I think that's a little dramatic, I just helped you to this room and checked your vitals after you collapsed. Hardly life saving," she argued.

"I insist. And so does my sister. You can tell my family how I came face to face with death tonight, but you saved me," and as I said it, a cold shiver ran down my spine.

"Are you sure? Really? They wouldn't mind? I mean, maybe just for a little," Nurse Glumly considered.

"Absolutely. My sister's car should be ready soon. When are you done here?" I asked.

"My shift was over two hours ago, but I just stayed. To help out. I... didn't want to rush home really," she said with a pained look.

My sister returned, and the three of us walked out the door. I found out Nurse Glumly's name was Kristen. We told her to just follow us to our grandmother's house, it wasn't far.

I had gone to donate blood in hopes of saving someone's life, but I guess I wasn't able to this time. No matter, it was almost time for a wonderful dinner at my grandmother's, and this year we'd share our traditions with Kristen.

***

Kristen got in her car, and started the engine. She put her cold hands in her coat pockets, and felt the note she had written that morning. She could feel the spots on the paper that had softened it as her tears fell, before she carefully folded it and had put it in her pocket for after work. She crumbled it up in her hand now, squeezing it tightly like Mr. Smiley was squeezed today. She took her small purse, and opened the glove box to throw it in as she always did. When she opened the box, her gun slid forward a little. She had put one bullet in it. That's all she needed. Slamming the box closed, she smiled. I mean, why not go for dinner. She hadn't eaten since she couldn't remember when, and who knows. Maybe Christmas Eve with this family would be nice. She thought about the other plan she had for tonight, and a chill crept down her spine.

She shifted into drive, and followed the little red car in front of her as the sun began to set. Not the ending she had planned this Christmas Eve. A wave of relief rushed through her.

A man dressed all in black leaned on his cane watching her pull away, before he disappeared into the night.

THE GINGERBREAD MAN

"*I don't want to go there...*" I whispered to nobody in the soft dim light of the Café, closing my eyes tight as if that could stop the memories from taking me back. I stopped, not five paces from the entrance, and knew I had to turn around and leave. I just wanted to run in for a coffee and danish on my way to work. The morning walk through the city was brisk and chilly, typical late November, yet steady streams of sunlight soaked into me. I'd felt happy and energized, until now.

The smell of gingerbread, warm and brown and sweet, filled the air. There was no way to stop it now. A gingerbread man had me by the hand and was dragging me back to my grandmother's kitchen.

"*I don't want to go there...*" I muttered again, turning around and making my way toward the door. But the gingerbread man tugged harder, he wouldn't let me go. He sat me at a small table near the door, and all of a sudden I was eight years old again. I closed my eyes, and the gingerbread man sat with me, asking me to remember. Swirls of cinnamon wrapped around my hair and arms, nutmeg and clove danced like glitter all around me. My grandmother was laughing, and I was straightening my blue checked apron that she had just tied. Gram had a matching one she wore. The white lace trim was itchy. Bing Crosby crooned about a White Christmas on the kitchen radio, a fixture on her counter next to the bread box adorned with yellow, orange, and brown flowers.

"Shall we make a whole army of gingerbread men?" she asked me.

"Yes!" I replied, and jumped down from the chair I'd been standing on. Mom would have yelled "Get down before you fall!", but Gram didn't mind. Gram knew I'd be ok.

I watched as she set the oven to preheat, then took

out cookie sheets. She never followed recipes, just knew what temperature and what ingredients came together like magic.

"Here's the spoon to mix with. I'll add everything slowly because it gets hard to stir. Then you can roll out the dough, and we'll cut out our army!" she told me.

I concentrated hard as I stirred the eggs that gooed slowly from their cracked shells, then the dark molasses that oozed from the measuring cup, then the sugar. There were puffs of white flour like clouds on the kitchen table. I paused and traced my name into a cloud, C-o-r-a, then I traced into another cloud G-r-a-m, with a heart around it.

Gram smiled, and gently took the bowl from me. I watched as her strong hands began to knead the thickening dough. Her skin was thin like rice paper, soft and smooth. I could see her blue veins rising like mountains through them.

"Can I try?"

"Of course, doll!" and she moved aside for me to step in. She always called me "doll", or "dolly", and it made me feel beautiful and special like a porcelain doll that was dearly loved and adored.

The dough was sticky, and it took all my might to squish it. I watched as it creeped through my fingers, brown slithering snakes coiling as they rose. I squished again, and patted it down flat. I balled my hands into fists like I'd seen Gram do, and pressed down hard, lifting my feet from the floor as I leaned into it.

"You're a natural at baking. You know just what to do," she gleamed. I proudly smiled back at her, wondering if it was the heat of the warming kitchen causing the glistening of sweat on her forehead.

"Time to roll!" Gram said, handing me the rolling pin.

I put my fingers gently into the bowl of silky soft flour, rubbing it against the smooth wood of the rolling pin. The marble handles were cold. The wood covered with flour felt a little course on my fingertips.

I began rolling the dough into an oval. It was really hard

to make it flat. My hands slipped a little on the handles of the rolling pin, and I tried to press it out from side to side.

"Would you like me to help?" Gram asked.

"Yeah, maybe a little," I said, and handed her the rolling pin.

Gram rolled the dough, her face getting more red as tiny beads of sweat were forming. Her thin blonde hair, recently permed into curls against her head, was darkened and sticking to her temples.

"Want me to do it, Gram?" I had asked.

"That's ok dolly, it's all ready now to cut out the army of gingerbread men!" she replied, using her apron to pat her wet face. Her breathing seemed heavy from all the rolling.

One by one, I pressed the shiny silver cookie cutter into the dough, releasing another soldier into the growing army of gingerbread men on the cookie sheets.

Once the army was at attention, all in a line, they were ready to be baked. Gram put them in the oven and glanced at the clock.

"Not long now, dolly. I'm just going to sit a little and rest my eyes. Keep an eye on them, ok?" she'd said, and sat in the kitchen chair. It was near the wall, and she rested her head back, closing her eyes.

I looked through the glass of the oven, tinged brown with age and use despite Gram's constant scrubbing. Slowly, the gingerbread men were starting to grow, to rise. The warmth of the oven caressed my face, the smell of cookies filled my nose, and Christmas music filled my ears.

"These smell so good, Gram!" I said, excited to see what they tasted like.

Gram didn't answer.

I turned around, and Gram didn't look well.

"Gram?" I yelled, trying to make her wake up.

Slowly, she opened her eyes, and gave me a weak smile.

"I'm not feeling that great right now, dolly. Call your mom, and ask her to come over. Tell her I might want the doctor to check on my heart. She'll know what to do."

"Ok, Gram, I'll call her," and I ran to the phone at the bottom of her steps. I dialed my number, poking my tiny finger into each numbered hole, spinning it in a circle and waiting as it spun back again before poking my finger into the next number.

"Mom, Gram isn't feeling right. She said to call and tell you the doctor needs to check her heart," I said as fast as I could.

"I'll be right there," my mom said before quickly hanging up.

I ran back to Gram.

"I think it's about time to get those gingerbread men out of there. Get the oven mitts and take them out. Put them on the counter. They can cool there," Gram said calmly.

I did as she said, and then my mom and dad hurried through the door.

"Mom, come with me. We'll go to the hospital to get you checked," my dad said. He helped Gram up.

"Cora. You stay here with your mom and get those gingerbread men decorated. I can't wait to see them when I get home," Gram said with a smile, then put her hand to her heart.

"I love you, sweetheart," she said and gave me a hug.

"I love you too, Gram. I'll decorate ALL of them! Wait til you see!" I said.

Dad and Gram left, and Mom and I finished up the cookies.

"Think Gram will be back soon?" I hopefully asked my mom, looking out the window. It had collected condensation on the inside from the heat of the cookies baking, but was now disappearing.

"Why don't we have some cookies while we wait for her. These are Gram's favorite to make. Let's try some," my mom coaxed.

"Ok. Gram is going to love how I put the icing on them!" I said, still expecting Dad and Gram to walk through the door any minute.

I sat on my mom's lap, eating gingerbread men and gazing out the window as the sky melted from blue to purple to black.

Gram never came back.

I felt something warm fall on my arm, and realized suddenly that I was crying, sitting alone in the Café. The smell of gingerbread continued to fill the air, and I saw a worker taking a tray from the oven, behind the counter.

Now the gingerbread man began to pull me in another direction. I wouldn't let myself think of Gram, of losing her, of anything that made me think of her. Maybe it was time to think of her again, he seemed to whisper gently. To talk to Dad about her, ask what she was like when he was a little boy. Did she bake gingerbread men with him? I'd buried all my feelings, squished them down like the gingerbread dough. It was time to let the memories creep up through my fingers, feel them, look at them.

I hadn't had gingerbread cookies since that day when my Gram, my best friend, left me forever. I wondered if it still tasted the same as that day.

The gingerbread man led me from the table. He urged me along, and seemed to say *"It's ok."* At the counter, I ordered a coffee and a gingerbread cookie, fresh from the oven with sweet white icing melting and dripping down its edges. It was warm in my hand, soft and a little cracked on top.

I went back to the small table by the door. I sat down and took a small bite of the still warm gingerbread. It was cinnamon, and ginger, and sugar, and molasses, and Christmas music, and white flour clouds that said Gram.

I took out my phone, and called Dad.

"Hey Dad. Have a minute?"

"Sure, sweetheart, what's up?"

"Tell me about Gram."

And I took another bite.

THE SURPRISE PARTY

Kerry checked and double checked the oven. She straightened her flower apron, took a breath, and opened the oven door. Almost ready now. Five more minutes, tops. Everything was going to be perfect. Perfect!

She floated to the island in the center of her freshly cleaned kitchen, and grabbed the knife. Sharp. So very sharp. Of course she always sharpened her knives, to get the most precise cuts. And the act of it was relaxing to her. The even rhythm of sliding a knife back and forth, this way that way this way that way, was satisfying to Kerry. She gazed at her reflection in the knife's metal and smiled. Deftly, she sliced cheese and arranged it carefully on the green plate already adorned with crackers.

Back to the oven, she removed the tray of hot puff pastries and set them to cool on top. The wine was chilling, the appetizers were just about ready, and fifteen minutes until the guests would arrive. And because it's a surprise for the guest of honor, she will arrive in 30 minutes. Today had been planned to the very minute! Months of preparation and thought went into how to execute the night flawlessly. And soon it would all pay off!

Kerry untied her apron and neatly folded it into the first drawer near the oven. She grabbed a bottle of Pinot from the refrigerator and helped herself to (another) glass. A job well done, she told herself!

Kerry had been friends with Amy fifteen years now. Ah, Amy. She touched the back pocket of her tight jean leggings where she had put her notes for the speech she was to make in Amy's honor tonight. She didn't want to miss a single thing!

"Everything looks great, hon!" Paul said from behind her. He walked into the kitchen, stole a piece of cheese, and put it wholly into his mouth.

"Thanks, sweetheart!" Kerry replied, taking another sip of wine.

"You always throw the best parties. What time will everyone be here?"

"We only have about 15 minutes before they should start arriving! It's really going to be a great night. It's been too long since everyone was able to make it. Dana has that new job, John is always traveling for work. Finally a night worked out for all our dear ones to come!" Kerry said with a smile.

"I'm going to change my shirt before they get here. Be right back." Paul said, and kissed Kerry on the cheek before disappearing upstairs.

Paul and Kerry were married 17 years. When they first married, Kerry worked at a bank full-time. Paul was in financing, and worked his way up to the top quickly. No longer "having" to work, Kerry quit her job and devoted her days to keeping house, volunteering for charities and the library, and tending her garden. Amy had asked her years ago if she ever became bored with the housewife life.

"I fill my time, believe me! There's always something to do." Kerry told her.
Paul wanted children. Most of their friends had children.

"It just wasn't meant to be." Kerry told her friends, family, and anyone who would listen.

The doorbell rang. The guests are arriving! Kerry hurriedly made her way to the door.

"They're here, Paul! They're here!" She shouted up the stairs.

"Greg! Lindsay! So glad you could make it!" Kerry said as she gave a quick hug to the first arrivals.

More and more friends arrived, until the house was buzzing with laughter and chatter. The wine flowed, the stories of past adventures, the warmth of love throughout the rooms.

Then, as 7pm approached, Kerry dimmed the lights in anticipation of Amy and her husband, Tom, arriving.

"Quiet! Quiet and gather in the dining room until I open the door!" Kerry laughed as she gave her instructions.

As she opened the door for Amy and Tom, Paul threw on the lights and everyone yelled "Surprise!" to the unexpecting couple.

"Oh you sneaky thing! How did you put this one past me? I had no idea!" Amy said as she hugged Kerry.

"I guess some of us are just good at secrets! Now, are you starting with wine or a cocktail tonight?" Kerry asked.

"I think the wine. Thank you!"

"And for you, Tom? A beer?" Kerry looked at Tom who was chatting with Paul.

"That would be great! Thanks!" he said.

She went to get the drinks, finishing off hers in the meantime. Kerry smiled as she gazed on her friends. It was almost time! But oh! The cake and presents! She mustn't forget those!

Kerry went to the kitchen and took the cake box from the refrigerator. She set it on the island, along with four candles. Now, where was the lighter? She checked the drawer and found it as Paul came in the kitchen.

"Need any help?" he asked?

"Oh, Paul! You startled me! I was lost in my thoughts. No, I have everything under control. Everything." Kerry said as she gathered several boxes from the counter. Wrapped in the prettiest paper, she couldn't wait to see their faces when they opened them!

Everyone always said Kerry threw the best parties, and gave the most thoughtful gifts. She took pride in knowing that she was good -really good- at some things.

Kerry placed the three small boxes atop the cake box, and made her way into the other room. Everyone was still laughing when she gently tapped her wine glass with a fork to get their attention.

"Everyone! Everyone it's time!" she said above the noise.

The room began to quiet, as everyone turned their attention to their hostess.

"Thank you everyone for coming tonight! It's been way too long since we've all been together like this! And what better reason than to celebrate Amy's birthday!"

A clapping and sound of glasses clinking bounced around the room.

"Now. You all know I've known Amy for what feels like forever at this point. But, how well do we really know a person? I think over the past few months I've been able to know her even better, as the hints and clues became more obvious! Like the new bathing suit you wore when we went to the pool! Perfect for a beach get-away! If nothing else, I'm observant, right?" Kerry looked around the room to smiling nodding faces.

"She must have bought them tickets for Jamaica! Or the Bahamas?" Dana whispered to John.

"What an awesome gift! A trip!" John whispered back.

"Which made picking out her present very easy for tonight! And, I even have one for Paul and Tom!" Kerry said as she picked up the boxes. She realized she didn't even need the notes she had made after all!

"Yep! Must be a vacation for them!" Jackie nudged Laura.

"They've talked about going for years! That Kerry, she ALWAYS has the best ideas!" Laura whispered.

"Ok ok, go ahead and open your boxes!" Kerry instructed.

The smiling trio opened their small matching boxes, and each took out a photo album. They all gave each other a quizzical look, then looked to Kerry.

"Oh! Those must be for the pictures they'll take on vacation!" Greg offered.

"Go ahead. Open them." Kerry said, with a smile that Laura tried to figure out.

They opened the albums to find them filled with pictures of Amy. And Paul. From the park, restaurants, the book store, Paul's office. Pictures of them holding hands. Kissing. And more. (Use your imagination.)

Kerry had known for months, though it appeared to have started years ago. She had followed them from a distance. Gotten proof.

Also in their boxes was a printout of texts Kerry had found under the name Andy in his phone. Clearly Amy. Receipts for lingerie that was never meant for Kerry. Even the receipt for Amy's new revealing bathing suit, charged to their joint credit card.

The blood drained from the three faces. The room fell silent. Mouths hung open.

"Who wants cake?" Kerry asked, holding up a knife and motioning to the cake she had just taken out of the box. On it, in edible photo paper, was an image she had snapped of Paul and Amy in an embrace kissing. Under it were written the words "It Was Never Meant to Be" in beautiful purple script icing.

Stunned, nobody knew what to do, so did nothing but look from Kerry to Amy to Paul to Tom and back to Kerry.

"Well. you all have your cake and eat it too. My bags are packed and waiting in the car. I do hope you all enjoyed the party! And…Surprise!" Kerry said as she walked out the door.

PINKY PROMISE

"Pinky promise?"

"Pinky promise."

I could hear our 8 year old voices in my head as I gazed out over the water from our bench. The pond was still, perfectly reflecting the white clouds that seemed to look the same as the day Alice and I made our promise, 30 years ago. A family of ducks glided near the shoreline, then climbed into the long damp grass that glistened in the sun. We used to chase the ducks together, feeding them bits of bread and crackers. Then they'd chase us. Alice and I would squeal and run, hopping on rocks and laughing.

"He's going to bite me! Wait, do ducks bite?" I'd asked, trying to hide the fear in my voice.

"Of course they bite! They have sharp teeth and maybe even venom!" Alice yelled from her rock. She was always the imaginative one, the adventurous one. She loved drama, and I was never sure if she found it or it found her. We were inseparable, so I was constantly apprenticed to her schemes and plans.

Growing up next door to Alice had meant we were more sisters than friends. My house was hers, hers mine. In the summer, we'd wander over in our pajamas for impromptu sleepovers, and play outside til the fireflies had to guide us home.

We swore graduation wouldn't change things. We'd go to college but visit all the time.

All the time became some of the time.

Some of the time became a few times a year.

Then...well life just happens. And distance grows. Until something unimaginable happens. Then the time and distance doesn't matter.

I realized I had walked closer to the water now. The soft ground began to swallow my shoes, dank sticky pond mud clinging to my sneakers. I laughed, as a memory tickled my brain.

"Will you be wearing your fancy sneakers tonight, or your casual ones?" Alice would always ask me. It didn't matter if we were going to the mall, the bar, or for a hike. I always wore sneakers.

I thought of the Missing Persons sign that was taking over the internet, all the local news stations, and the national news. "Missing Person: Alice Barker, Last seen wearing black leggings, purple hoodie, and black sneakers. Contact Danmore Police Department with any information."

What was she doing going for a walk by herself? She knew it would get dark. She knew she would be taking a risk. But, I suppose that was just Alice. She was invincible. And I prayed she was.

They say that every minute matters in a missing persons case. It had been...more than 48 hours now I think. I thought about getting the call from my mom.

"Sweetheart, I have some bad news. Alice hasn't been home, and everyone is worried. I think you should come here. I don't have a good feeling about this."

And with that, I jumped in my car and began the four hour drive back to our town, and back to the one place I thought would give me clarity. The place we had made our promise 30 years ago.

"This is our pond. Whenever we need each other, we meet here. Not my house or your house or anywhere else. Deal?" Alice had insisted, our pinkies locked almost as tightly as our eyes.

"Pinky promise?"

"Pinky promise."

It was a deal as good as legally binding in our world. And if there were ever a time we needed each other, it was now. Why had she gone on that walk all alone? And why hadn't I called her in months? I tried to think of the last time I'd heard her voice. And then, I heard a voice.

"Knew I'd find you here."

The voice from behind me was unmistakable. I knew before turning the face that belonged with that voice that belonged with me.

"Alice!" I screamed as I turned around, tears in my eyes. She knew to come back to our spot, to our pond. It was as if the weight of the world had been lifted, and I had been given a second chance at our friendship. A second chance to make right the years that had been lost to college, and jobs, and families, and travel, and life. There's never enough time, unless you make the time. I looked at my best friend, and smiled at her. She was smiling right back at me, and I didn't know if I should hug her or chastise her for worrying everyone, for worrying me.

"Alice, I can't believe it's you! I was so worried about you! Everyone was! Girl, what happened? Why were you gone so long? God am I happy you're back though!" I said as I hugged her.

"Nora, I knew you'd be here! I knew you'd remember our promise!"

"Of course I would!" I laughed.

"I was so scared, Nora. I don't know why I did it. I wanted to get away, clear my head. I had so much going on," Alice said as the smile faded and hurt filled her brown eyes.

"I'm so sorry I didn't even know that. I should have been a better friend to you. I should have called, messaged, anything. I let you down," I tried to apologize.

"No, it was both of us. But now, here we are. And we can figure out this new adventure, just like we figured out all our other adventures," Alice said.

"Our new adventure?" I asked, not knowing the crazy plan my best friend now seemed to have up her sleeve, just as we were reunited.

"Well, yeah. You do know, don't you?" Alice asked, looking at me quizzically.

"Know? Know what?" I asked, not understanding.

Alice took my hands in hers.

"You don't know, do you. Nora, I didn't make it. It got dark when I was out walking. A man came…he…came from behind. I was so scared. But then it was all over."

"What are you talking about, Alice? I don't understand."

"And when you came to find me. Nora, you were driving too fast. You were scared too, and worried, and never saw the curve or the tree…But I saw it all."

"What are you saying, Alice?" I was trying to piece it all together. I looked at my friend. And looked through my friend. Oh, my God…

"We're dead, Nora. But we both knew to come here. We knew that this is where we needed to go. It will be ok, Nora," Alice said, reassuring me.

"Pinky promise?"

"Pinky promise."

BECOMING INVISIBLE

Georgia was six. Straw colored hair, blue raspberry popsicle eyes. Sometimes they melted, and tiny drops would speckle her pink unicorn shirt. But mostly, she was happy to play in the dirt and slide at the park with a smile that wrapped from one purple earring to the other. Sometimes she had a bow in her hair, but too often it would just fall out as she ran around from one adventure to the next. And today she had braids that kept her hair from her face. Always exploring, always curious. She was so much like me at that age. Until I wasn't.

My view becomes hazy as a memory forms behind my eyes. Six years old. The light creeping in from beneath the closet door I was hiding in. The sound of something smashing. A glass? A vase? Shards bounced then settled as the screaming got louder. A door slammed. The front door. I think he's gone. I hear the car engine try to start. And again. I realize I haven't breathed in a few minutes. I take a breath slowly and silently. It's not ok to come out yet. It's not ok to come out yet. The engine fires and I hear tires as angry as my father screech away into the night. What time is it? I wasn't sure. I'd gone to bed, heard the sound of yelling and crying, and ran to my spot. The spot he can't find me. Where the darkness makes me invisible. I want to stay invisible. I hug my knees close to me, shut my eyes, and wait. Always waiting in the dark for the light. I blink away my thoughts and return to now. I return to the little girl who has the same straw colored hair as me.

I take her hand and smile, nodding toward the swings. She's so trusting, so very innocent because the world has been rainbows for her. She drops the stick she was drawing with in the dirt.

"This is my favorite dirt. It's the softest at the park!" she tells me, and runs cheerfully to the lowest swing she could climb on. Futile attempts at pumping her legs to gain air were reflected in the frustration on her face. She was determined to do it herself, to be independent. But then became impatient, as most children her age tend to do.

"Push me!" she giggled as I made my way over.

"Of course! Hang on tight!" I said as I gave her a gentle shove forward, then let go of my hands to watch her glide back again.

"Higher!" she demanded. And I happily complied.

"Higher!" he said, as he watched me put the boxes on the shelf. I close my eyes and see my manager, standing too close behind me, at my first job when I was a teen. Another memory hits me before I can stop it. Stop it! I can't stop it, I can't stop them from coming. I'm back in the grocery store, shelving cereal, and I feel his eyes on me. Always on me.

"That's it, sweetheart. Right there." he whispers, his hot breath coating my ear and sticking to it. I cringe and try to sink into the shelving in front of me. He likes to make me reach to the top shelves, telling me I don't need the stepstool. Just stretch those long arms, he orders.

"Why don't you take that sweater off. It's pretty hot today, and you'll be much cooler. I have a lot more boxes for you to put away before we close. You should get comfortable," and he reached out to slide my cardigan off my shoulders. His forehead practically touched mine, and I backed away, into the shelf behind me. His hands went under my sweater, onto my shoulders as he tried to take it off me.

"No, that's ok. I'm usually cold," I said and sidestepped away from him.

Not much older than me, he was made manager because everyone else left that job. He was the only one who stayed well after he graduated high school when all the others went to college.

"It's not my thing, sweetheart," he told me one night as I was scheduled with him to close. I usually tried to avoid him, but that night he decided to tell me about why he chose to stay and work rather than go to college. As if I cared what his life goals were. He touched my arm and said he'd locked the door in the front. He asked me to check in the back that the rear door was locked too.

"Yes, I'll go check," I said.

"Yes '*sir*', you'll go check," he frowned.

"Yes, *sir*, I'll go check," I dutifully replied.

I needed this job. I needed a way to get out of my house. And this was how I would do it. Even if it meant being obedient. I had learned early on that being quiet and obedient was best. Just be a good girl and listen.

He smiled as I walked away. I went to the back, and placed my hand on the cold metal knob that opened into the night on the other side. It was summer. If I had friends, I probably would have been meeting up with them after work to hang out. Maybe see a movie, or go to a party. That's what teenagers did for fun, right? Went to each other's houses, drove to the woods and made a campfire to sit and drink until curfew. My parents never gave me a curfew because they were never home themselves. Sometimes they wouldn't come home for days, and once they were gone for over a week. They never called to tell me where they were. But if I'm honest, I was happier when they were gone. I never wanted to be like them. Never.

I turned the knob slightly and felt that it was locked. Before I could turn to go back, I felt myself being slammed into the door, held in place by an arm at my neck and body at my back. "You won't tell, sweetheart," he ordered. That was the first time. It certainly was not the last time. And I told no one, just as he said. I *had* no one.

"Higher!" Georgia's shout brought me back to the park. Back and forth, the pendulum child swung. Like my thoughts. Back and forth. I wondered if there were swings at the elementary school she would be attending in the Fall. Kindergarten. I wondered if there would be anyone there to push her. But that was weeks away from now. Still weeks upon weeks to drink in the summer. I had missed the registration date, but that didn't matter. I spoke with the secretary and found out I could register anytime. All I needed was the necessary documents. And those were already made and ready to go.

We'd been to this park daily it seemed. I watched her climb the stairs to the slide gingerly at first, slowly going down and stopping completely to carefully get off at the bottom. As the days moved on, that hesitation disappeared and she was bouncing down as fast as she could with a leaping dismount into the rubber mulch. She gained confidence, and threw proud smiles at the other children who were not as daring as she had become. She said she's going to teach her baby brother that it's ok to be scared at first, but to be brave. A toddling one-year-old who already looked up to her. You can see it in his face as he watches her play. His hair is darker than hers, an almond brown. It suits him.

Georgia jumps off the swing as it sails upwards, spreading her arms like a butterfly into the sky. She seems to hang suspended in the air for a moment until gravity wins, and she tumbles onto the ground laughing. I can't help but laugh with her.

"Are you ok, little bird?" I ask as she meets my gaze. Her right knee is scraped, but she doesn't seem to care. The tiniest speck of red appears, and she wipes it away.

Red runs down my face, and I wipe it away. He laughs and calls me a whore, zipping up his pants as he walks to the fridge to get a beer. My wedding night. The memory slams me in the face like his hands did so many times. And I wiped the blood and kept quiet. It didn't start with blood and beatings. It was beaches and books. Breakfasts in bed.

Then it wasn't.

I learned it had been an act, a sober charade. When his drinking was uncontrolled, so was he. He was a successful dentist, and had his own practice where he employed others to take on his clients when he didn't show up. He was surprisingly good at dentistry, and that's what made him a success despite his frequent missed appointments.

"Another emergency for Dr. Collins, I'm afraid. I'll be working on you instead today," his employees would cover.

"If anyone can handle an emergency, it's Dr. Collins! Give him my best when you see him," they would say.

The truth decay inside his mouth didn't just extend across his practice, but across everyone around him. And that's how I was fooled into a quick marriage only a few months after meeting him. Maybe if I had waited, I would have seen him. Really seen him.

The first time I saw him, he was running through the park I always went to for fresh air while I read. I glanced up, noted his muscular arms and legs, then returned to my book. I didn't dream to think he would notice me.

Yet, the next day, he did.

I was on my usual bench under the tree so the sun wouldn't shine brightly on the pages of my book. Lost in the world of Austen, I didn't hear him approach from behind. I'm not sure how long he stood there feigning a stretch before I turned around.

"Anything good?" he asked, his eyes flashing to my book.

"Yes, if you like Austen," I replied with a nervous smile. The look on his face said he had not heard of Austen, but he smiled and sat down next to me.

"Austen's great. Yeah, I really like his work. Deep stuff."

I looked at him with a raised brow, but before I could say anything, he asked me to dinner the following night. It was a tornado from there.

Eventually, I learned to count the empty cans in the trash to gauge how soon to disappear for a while.

Finally, I just disappeared.

I had gotten good at picking up and leaving, taking only what I needed. I did it when I was a teenager and escaped my father. I did it after having more black eyes and bruises than I could bear any more. I smiled at the thought of becoming so good at becoming invisible. Like in the closet as a child. Just be quiet and disappear...

"Again!" Georgia yells as she picks herself up off the ground, and gets back on the swing. She is looking to me in a request to push her again.

I look around, and know it's time.

"Ok, but first, how about that ice cream? We better get there before they close for the day!" I say and hold out my hand.

"Yay! Ice cream time!" Georgia squeals and races over to me. I take her small hand, still covered in dirt from earlier. We walk to the car, and I help her into the booster seat that I have secured in the back seat. Next to her seat, several books lay in a neat pile. And near those, several coloring books and crayons. A sippy cup and snack bag of goldfish catch her eye, and she excitedly tells me she loves goldfish. As if I didn't already know that, and bought them especially for today.

As we leave the parking lot, I look back in my rearview mirror. I see Georgia's mom and baby brother walk out of the bathrooms where she was changing him. She looks around. She's probably saying "See Georgia? That only took a minute!"

And that's all I needed.

RESIGNED

Frederick Tuftman
Resignation Letter

August 23, 2023
Barbara McGraw, Head of Human Resources
Crane Industries
3425 Industrial Way, Mooreville, West Virginia
(503) 555-8240

To Whom It May Concern,

And, we all know, this concerns everyone. So feel free to share this via group email, or I would really recommend a PowerPoint presentation where you can add photos and music. That's a great idea. (Do they ever end with me? No, they don't.) I'd recommend Laura in Business Affairs handle it. She's the best with this type of thing, and my exit deserves nothing less than the best, as I'm sure we would all agree upon.

I would like to formally announce my last day of employment with Crane Industries to occur on Friday, September 8, 2023. This should allow ample time for the Party Planning Committee to arrange the catering and entertainment for my Farewell Luncheon. (I'm looking at you, Debbie. Don't skimp on the hors d'eouerves like you did at Becky's Baby Shower.)

I have given longer than the customary two weeks notice in order to be fully appreciated for my time here. Also, Jeff in Accounting won't be back from vacation until the last Thursday of August and he will want to know and prepare for my departure. He still owes me lunch from that time in 2021 he lost his credit card for three days. I bought him a Philly Cheesesteak with everything, a Diet Coke, and a side of curly fries. I have the receipt should it be needed. This should also be plenty of time for Sue to pick out a large card for everyone to sign with their favorite memories of working with me. And Sue, don't add cash to the card from everyone. Take a collection then include a variety of Gift Cards to my favorite local restaurants. Gerry will know which ones. I've told her all of my favorites over the years.

It has been a pleasure to work for such a company as Crane Industries. Though, the pleasure has all been yours, I'm most sure. Never has an employee been early for work three years in a row, without so much as a sick day taken. Neither stomach bug nor flu could hold me back. (Sorry again about your desk, Ronnie. You really should request an area further away from the bathrooms.)

My greatest contributions, however, will be the legacy I leave in aesthetic efforts for the betterment of the company. The Frederick Tuftman Nature Reserve, located between the parking lot and front door, has grown exponentially in size and beauty over the years. Once the Placard was installed, I personally planted 8 Gerber Daisies. And when they died (they're so temperamental - like Marcy in Finance. Don't invite her to the Farewell Luncheon), I replaced them immediately with plastic ones that can't die. Then came the gnomes, plastic ferns, and bird bath. And being the clever man that I am, I had the foresight to drill holes in the bird bath so as to not collect water and attract birds and their messes. Terribly dirty creatures, birds.

And now the moment of clarity, the moment I reveal the reason for my untimely and unexpected departure from those who love me so dearly at Crane. When I was a child, my parents revealed to me that I was, in fact, "gifted". It's not something I share often, as it serves only to intimidate others. They avoid me, refrain from inviting me to social gatherings, and block my number from their phones. I fear my secret has been revealed here at Crane. There can be no other explanation for the repeated attempts of avoidance. It has happened at my last five places of employment, so it really comes as little surprise that alas, it has happened again. My brain is my cross to bear. I've learned that filing discrimination suits against my employers and coworkers will not resolve anything. It is always best that I instead find new employment. And, I do have to say, my employers have always provided recommendations of my skills and abilities that glow brighter than a super moon on a warm summer's night. It's as if they are so extremely torn by my decision to leave, that they do everything in their power to secure alternate employment for me.

And now, upon my leave, I would like to bestow my heartfelt thanks to several coworkers. Dave, in Accounts Receiving, always found time to compliment my hair when I had it cut. I know everyone else noticed, but Dave was the only one not jealous enough to tell me how fantastic I looked.

Cindy, in Local Sales, shared her milk in the employee lounge for my coffee every day. She didn't know it, but now she does.

Jen at Reception always forwarded my calls, even when the person claimed they were on vacation or out of office. We always got them eventually, didn't we Jen?

And finally, Lou in Maintenance. Every time my ID badge glitched and wouldn't let me into the building (which was quite often- someone really needs to fix the main door), Lou would set down his mop, shake his head in frustration that he had to let me in again, and come to my rescue.

As I read once at a restaurant exit, "parting is such sweet sorrow" (credit Applebees), but the time has come for me to move on and forge a new path. I have no doubt my skills, experience, and abilities will be more than appreciated elsewhere. I offer my condolences to you, my colleagues, at your loss. You will never again have the extreme fortune of working with a truly Gifted Individual, as evidenced by the report my mother has in a file somewhere. You will continue on at Crane, but your lives will be lacking in many ways. There will be a dark void where I had once provided light.

I do invite all of you to reach out at any time and communicate with me. I hold no grudges, I burn no bridges. You cannot be held to blame for your natural instinct to fear the most intellectually superior amongst the group. It's science.

My transition out of the company will not be easy, but I have faith in you, my former colleagues. I suggest Covered Dish Wednesday be moved to Monday the 11th to give everyone a reason to go in knowing I'll be gone.

Most Sincerely,

Frederick Tuftman

NO STARS FOR YOU

Luigi's Palatable Palace   0.0/5 Stars
Frederick T. *said*:

"I consider myself a food connoisseur. I grew up eating three meals a day. I often made my own breakfast cereal, with a range of milk choices to complement the selection. For example, always use a 2% with Raisin Bran. Almond milk goes best with Cheerios, while whole milk is definitely the best with Rice Chex. Shredded Wheat: just throw that straight in the bin. Nobody should eat that garbage with any kind of milk. Why am I sharing my expertise? I feel you should be aware of my level of experience with food before I shred the wheat of your establishment.

Let me present my <u>Menu of Disgust</u> with your "fine dining restaurant", as Yelp falsely classifies you.

Beverage: only Pepsi products as a fountain drink choice? First mistake. Coke products are, and always will be, superior to Pepsi products. I could get into the history of the products, but I'll save that for our face-to-face meeting (I'm in the process of arranging with corporate). My PowerPoint presentation will make it quite clear, as well as the three zany TikTok reels I made that I'll share for good measure. Back to the subpar soda. The ratio of ice to liquid was completely off. It should ideally be a 60/40 split. Yours was closer to 10/90. I have proven in timed experiments that the rate at which ice melts on average over the course of a meal must coincide with this ratio so as to not leave one with a watered down beverage by the time appetizers are finished. My studies and findings are published, if you wish you read further. (I'll send you my Facebook, Insta, and Twitter links where you can find my posts about it. There are MANY comments from people who "like" and agree with me.)

Appetizer: Or, should I say, UNappetizer. I ordered chicken wings. I like my wings hot, crispy, full of delectable meat, and with a reasonable amount of heartburn expected. (I carry my own antacid in anticipation of acid distress.) What I was served appeared to be the plucked and fried wings of a hummingbird. Is it even legal to serve fried hummingbird wings? I highly doubt it. I'll look into that one, and you may be hearing from PETA as well.

Main course: I ordered the "Fresh haddock entree", described as being sautéed with olive oil, garlic, and fresh tomatoes. When the waitress brought the dish, I was sure there was a mistake.

"Excuse me, madam, but I did not order the tomato soup!" I told her.

She assured me "on her grandpappy's grave" mind you, that it WAS the fresh haddock dinner entree. I looked again at the preposterous pesce placed in front of me. I was able to see what appeared to be several white islands of fish swimming in the tomato soup. Where were the fresh tomatoes? Was the olive oil really snake oil?? The whole meal a farce?
I tried it anyway. I have an adventurous appetite and spirit, therefore I was willing to give pesce a chance. I swirled the soup, stabbed a white bit of flesh, and placed it precariously in my mouth. Immediately, I was hit with what tasted like salty sadness. If you took the disappointment of losing a race, the sadness of waking up on Christmas morning with socks and underwear instead of a video game, the anxiety of failing a test, and put them all in a bowl that would be this meal. I do believe your chef may very well have emptied a bottle of ketchup into a saucepan, added fish, and proclaimed it a meal. Well, sir, let me tell you in my loudest voice it was horrendous. This meal should not be given to the likes of man nor beast. Pigs would scoff at this slop in a trough. If you advertise a "Fresh Haddock", you best not

deliver it in ketchup soup.

Dessert: after the wholly traumatizing experience of the main course, I needed recourse. I needed to cleanse my palate of the assault to my gustatory faculties. Then, I saw it. Tiramisu. It literally MEANS "cheer me up". And that's exactly what I needed at this point. Heavenly caffeine in the espresso, delicate sweetness in the lady fingers, a touch of cocoa, and BAM! My whole dining experience had the potential to be turned around. The fate of this review rested in a 4x4 square of decadence on a dessert plate. My mouth salivated as I looked at it. My FitBit reinforced the fact that my heart rate was indeed rising in anticipation of the sweet reward in front of me. I steadied myself, swished some water, bit the lemon that wedged high upon its glass. The sour garnish served to cleanse my palate before diving into that divine dessert. I searched the square for the exact location of "the perfect bite". It must include the lady fingers, the ganache, the cocoa topping in all the right proportions. Like a pirate seeking treasure, a veritable X marked the spot dead center where my fork was set to dig. I carved out the piece, closed my eyes to diminish my other senses, and put it in my mouth. I chewed, I moved the sweet bolus from left to right to left again. I swallowed. I gagged! What was THIS???? In the center of my Tiramisu was the unmistakable remnants of broccoli florets! No vegetable has ANY business in, near, or incorporated into a dessert! Your pastry chef should be ashamed of this endeavor! The beauty of the Tiramisu can NOT be enhanced by the addition of vegetables, no matter what sort of health advantage it may have. Is this part of that Keto diet fad? To sell more "unhealthy" dessert by marketing it as "healthy" due to the addition of broccoli? I am appalled. I am disgusted. I am requesting a refund. (Please see attachment with bill and proof of payment.)

Dining Conclusion: Based on the grievances addressed above, I have no choice but to withhold any positive feedback. No stars for you.

Signed: *Frederick Tuftman*

CRAZY CATE

I never asked to be paired with Cate. The community center randomly threw us together with no apparent reasoning, other than we were around the same age.

When my mom suggested I get a job with the Township that summer, I groaned and watched my days of reading outside in the grass under a tree evaporate like a puddle on a sunny day.

"You'll have plenty of time to read and be lazy until school starts again. I think you'll like it," she prodded.

"Fine. I'll apply, but if I DON'T get it, I can't say I'll be sorry," I told her as I slunk from the kitchen and up to my room.

To my mother's delight and my disappointment, I was hired. Even worse, I could start immediately. I was to report to the Township Community Center the following Monday to receive my assignment. Would I be assigned Game Coordinator in the Rec building? Trash collector along the streets? Pool Concession stand worker at the Community Pool? I didn't want to get my hopes up for any of the positions available that some town director doled out to hapless teens looking for summer jobs. I envisioned getting pelted with dodgeballs in the Rec room, and burning pizza slices at the pool. My preferred tasks were reading and eating popsicles in the summer sun. I decided whatever I was assigned would just be terrible. End of story.

That Monday, I rode my bike to the Community Center, and dropped it in the lawn out front. I went into the mildly air conditioned building and found the reception desk.

"I'm here to get my job placement for the summer. Where should I go?" I asked the girl manning the desk. She didn't bother to look up from her Teen Magazine as she told me conference room B. Down the hall. The OTHER hall. (My sense of direction was as lacking as my other skills).

I found conference room B and gently opened the door to

peek inside. A handful of teens, dripping sweat and hormones, filled the tiny room. Everyone turned at once to look at me, and I felt my face redden as I tried to strut as nonchalantly and coolly as I could to the bulletin board listing our names and assignments.

There it was.

Rachel Roberts - Parks and Recreation Craft Committee

What the heck was a craft committee job? There was no description. I saw everyone still staring at me, so I applied a mask of teenage apathy and turned to them and shrugged.

"Craft committee. Whatever."

I waited to see if they bought it. They all returned the apathetic shrug, gave a nod, and went back to their chatter.

I was relieved to be out of the spotlight, and just as I began to let out a sigh of relief, the door swung open in alarming ferocity and spit through it none other than Crazy Cate Collins. Crazy Cate burst into the room like a firework set to explode at any minute. She let out a "Hey ya'll!" and ran to the Corkboard of Fate and (Mis)Fortune, as I was about to find out my summer would be tangled up in Crazy Cate's erratic life.

"Craft Committee! Yes!" she shouted, and pumped her fist. She then ran around the room like an NFL receiver who'd just scored the winning touchdown of the game smacking everyone with high-fives.

Wait. Craft Committee? With..me?! I knew it had to be a mistake. I couldn't possibly be paired with that pariah.

But no. There it was. Plain as the frown on my face. Cate and I were both assigned Craft Commitee for the summer.

"Who did I get this year?" Cate asked and scanned the room. Nobody replied, but I could practically see the thought bubbles dancing above all their heads saying "thank goodness not me!"

I slowly lifted my head, took a step forward, and accepted my fate with Cate.

"It's me. I'm on Craft Commitee too," I about whispered.

"Well, Worm, looks like it's you and me this summer! Saddle up, it's going to be a wild ride!" she laughed.

"Worm? Actually, my name's..." I started.

"Bookworm! I know who you are. And listen, no books allowed on the job, ya hear me? We have serious crafting to do!" she feigned a serious face.

It was worse than I thought. No lazy summer reading, AND paired with Crazy Cate making crafts? I never wanted school to start more vehemently than I did at that moment.

"Well, let's get our supplies and get to it!" she said as she grabbed me by the arm and dragged me out the door. Good gracious, was she a weight lifter too? My little arm throbbed in her massively strong grip, as I urged my feet to move faster to keep up with her.

"This here's the closet we get our supplies before we start each day. We choose a craft, go to one or two parks in town each day, and the little lemmings come over to us and make something. Got it, Worm?" she asked.

"Um, yeah. Got it. Um...how do you know all this already?" I asked quietly.

"I was craft committeed by these clowns last summer too. I know it inside and out. How to work, how to LOOK like you're working, and the best places in town to hide out til work's over. Stick with me, Worm, and you'll be in for the best time of your sorry life!" she promised.

Sounded more like a prison sentence. And I was about to commence with Day 1.

We grabbed the craft boxes and carried them outside to her car. I use the term loosely. It had an engine, some doors, and it moved. But I felt like I should be signing some kind of waiver before getting inside: "I hereby relinquish all rights to life while traveling from point A to point B" or something of the sort.

"Get inside, Worm!" Cate ordered.

I obeyed, wide-eyed and terrified.

The car smelled of some kind of alcohol and I was pretty

sure a family of skunks had made a home under the driver's seat.

"First we can go to Memorial Park. It's pretty empty Mondays. We can lay low there awhile," Cate commiserated.

On the way, Cate told me we just had to tell the township folks which parks, which days, and how many kids crafted that day. A purely made-up magical number not-too-high, not-too-low, just right to keep us in "business".

And so it was.

For the duration of the summer, Cate and I went park hopping with our craft supplies. She would disappear into the woods with a backpack of bottles, like bait for the "cool kids" who followed her in. The pied-piper of delinquents.

I'd sit at the picnic tables and benches waiting for any kids that wanted to craft, with instructions to tell our boss Mr. Carter she was just in the bathroom with "lady troubles" should he show up for a spot check to make sure we were crafting. That excuse always caused him enough awkward discomfort to slow down his checks on us.

I began to worry about how much and how often Cate got into drinking and drugs. She always managed to be well enough by the end of the day to drive us back to the center to return the supplies and for me to get my bike to ride home.

But I feared it didn't stop when she got home. And it started getting worse as the days drew near to summer's end.

"Mom? Can I talk to you about something?" I had started one day. I needed advice. I needed to know if I should talk to Cate about what I was seeing.

"Yeah, Sweetheart? What is it?" My mom asked with a smile on her face.

"Um, did you wash my red tank top yet? I wanted to wear it tomorrow," I chickened out.

"Yeah, it's in your room. Was that all?" my mom suspiciously asked.

"Yep! Thanks!" I said and ran off. Bock Bock Bock.

I was still debating how I could bring up the topic the next day, when Cate slung her backpack over her perfectly tanned shoulders and got ready to disappear again for the day.

"Alright, Worm, hold down the fort and man the glitter til I get back!" she said with a salute of her hand in my direction. And then she was gone. Again.

Hours later, she still hadn't come out from the woods. Not entirely unusual for her, but I suddenly had a feeling in my gut I should go look for her.

I left my glue and popsicle sticks, and went to the tree line where she had gone in. It was eerily quiet. I called out a few times, but without an answer. I could feel the sweat running down my back as I began to worry more.

As I walked further into the woods, my shoes crunched the leaves of last Fall, soon to be replaced with the leaves of this Fall. I looked down the path ahead, and saw something. I hurried closer and found a very pale, very unconscious Cate.

I tried to wake her up, but she was out. I ran from the woods as fast as I could to the pay phone by the bathrooms. I rummaged through my Jean shorts pockets and found coins, then called 911 breathlessly as my hands shook and my heart punched my chest.

I told the dispatcher what had happened, where to send an ambulance, and then ran to the road to guide them to the woods when they arrived.

I remember watching them take Cate on a stretcher out of the woods, and into the ambulance. I remember watching it pull away, screaming sirens cutting the hot summer silence. I don't know how long I'd been crying at that point, but I sank to the ground and sobbed then. Full body, shaking crying.

An EMT had called my mom to pick me up, and I went home and just sat with her. Crying, worrying, and wishing Cate would be ok. Mom tried to make me feel better, told me I'd done the right thing. Did I?

I finished out the next week by myself at the parks. I wondered how Cate was doing, and if she was still in the hospital.

When school started, I heard a rumor Cate was in rehab

and wouldn't be back for awhile. I wondered if she was mad at me for calling the ambulance. Maybe she would have been fine and woken up? Maybe I overreacted? I couldn't shake the feeling that maybe I got her in trouble and she would never forgive me. And everyone at school wouldn't forgive me either for jumping the gun and ruining Cate's summer when all she wanted to do was have fun. These thoughts consumed me for weeks.

I was still trying to push those thoughts away when I stopped for a drink at the water fountain after Science. As I stood up, I looked down the hall and saw her. It was Cate. She was back. And she was walking straight towards me. I tried to read her face, and couldn't. Was she mad? Would she even acknowledge me? She looked so much better than she had in the summer. Her tan was long gone, but her face looked healthier. Her eyes weren't sunken in and rimmed with darkness.

As she grew close, she gave me a nod.

"Hey, Worm. Thanks."

And with that, she walked by me and greeted her friends who were waiting down the hall.

That summer, I had begrudgingly taken on my first job. It was the summer of Crazy Cate, crafts, and coming to learn that there are going to be tough decisions in life. And you may second guess yourself, and your actions. But sometimes you just have to trust your gut, and give a little grace to others as they learn about their decisions too.

MIRROR|MIRROR

Raki looked at the drying blood on his hands, and decided it was time. This life was not the one he'd imagined, and every day it's been more and more difficult to continue the ruse living in Drassai. Shadows of his past kept creeping up, and he was becoming the former Raki. Scared, timid, spineless.

He sat on the front step of the house, picked at the blood, and wiped his hands on his equally bloodied pants. His hand felt the gun in his pocket as he again tried to clean his actions from his shaking body. He did not remember where the gun came from. Was it stolen? Given to him? Is he the type of person now to steal on top of everything else? He decided he must have brought it with him. He must have had it all along. Didn't he?

It was just becoming morning. The sun was slowly emerging behind the snow capped mountains in the distance. There would be fallout soon. They'd know what happened. Everyone would know. There would be a SkyWrite announcing to everyone that a killer was on the loose. A killer. Was that really what now defined him? On the other side, he was a mild mannered office worker. But here...

Raki stood and began to make his way to the tree line before the mountains. It was time.

Drassai was not yet awake, there were no people on the street to block his way or question him. He ran through what had happened over and over in his mind. There was no moving on from it here. He thought of Jesa, the woman he fell in love with, the woman who made him come alive. He was a different person here. It was as if coming through the mirror from his world, to Drassai, had changed him. He no longer felt inhibited here. He no longer felt the constant pressure of anxiety crushing him. He was light, free, adventurous, and...a killer.

He hadn't been back to his world since coming to Drassai

nearly a year ago. But time moved differently here. He became accustomed to it, played the part of a native here, and sold it. It wasn't easy, but he'd convinced everyone he was no different than they.

Jesa never suspected a thing. He'd met her right away, and it was an instant connection. He'd never dated anyone before, but he felt a new confidence here to pursue her. But then, then she ruined it all.

Raki learned that in Drassai, there were no rules about relationships. Be with one, be with one hundred, anything was fine. Raki had hoped Jesa would be different than the others. That she'd only want him. But then Jesa met Grafeur.

Strong, charismatic Grafeur. Looking at him was like seeing the antithesis of himself. And Jesa was not just enamored, but completely devoted to him.

And now, there was a body. And blood. And guilt.

Raki could see the mirror reflecting the early sun's light in the distance. He would leave this life behind. He stepped closer to the mirror. He prepared himself to walk through, back to his home. He paused, and looked up. Staring back at him was not the face of Raki...it was Grafeur. Confused, he put his hands on his face. Hands that were...free of blood? He noticed movement behind him. It was Jesa, making her way towards him with a smile on her face. It wasn't Grafeur he'd killed...it was Raki.

TARGET(ED)

"LIZZZZ! Liz! Hey!"

I stopped in my tracks as that high pitched voice invaded my unprepared eardrums. The drawn out zzzz was like a nest of hornets swarming my head. I recognized that voice. I debated running. Hiding. I could slip down the housewares aisle and pretend I didn't hear her. Stoop down low and really investigate the specifications on a coffee maker. Something. Anything.

Nope. Too late. She was now jog-running at me. I could hear her quickening steps and knew it was now unavoidable. I took a deep breath and tried to fill my lungs with zen and sunshine.

Ugh. I turned and made my "surprised" face. It was Carolynn with two "n"s. She was dressed in fashionable workout clothes, her hair on point, not a smudge anywhere in her perfect make-up. Do women like her sweat?

"Carolynn! Oh my GOODNESS!" I said, trying to match the bar she had set in decibel level.

Her jog-run did not slow down. I took a step back. Oh no, was she going to hug me? She was! I felt like a human target, unable to avoid this impending arrow aimed at me flying faster and faster. Her noodle arms flung around me and I immediately stiffened like a corpse at a wake. I'm not a hugger. I don't like touching. I started to sweat. Is it rude to push someone off you? Before I could bring my hands up to remove her lilac scented body from mine, she had stepped back to examine me.

"Liz! You look wonderful! What have you been UP to? Gosh, it's been years!" She said with a smile so white-bright beaming at me that I felt like I was being interrogated by the cops under a truth-lamp.

"Oh, you know. Working. The kids, their activities, it just never ends, you know? What about you? You look amazing!" I crooned at her. Was I smiling? I flexed my mouth muscles and hoped it wasn't overly Cheshire.

"Oh, do I? I'm just a mess today! I was just at the gym, then stopped for my latte, and realized I should probably stop here and grab all the things I DON'T need! Isn't that always how it is here?" Carolynn said with a laugh so hard (fake) that she doubled herself over ever-so-slightly as she awaited my reaction. She continued to smile at me as she looked up through her thick black fake eyelashes perfectly glued to her eyes. They looked like little furry hamsters resting themselves for a spell.

"Yes, well, I mostly came for laundry detergent." I shrugged and began inching myself further back from the conversational onslaught of forced socialization.

"Do you remember Amy? Amy from high school? She was dating Mark back then, but then got married to Dave, and well THAT was a disaster! I just saw they are now the big D officially and I HEARD it was because he was cheating! Can you believe that? Well I sure can. I never liked him you know. Not even in high school. She can do so much better. Oh, are you still married? How's Bill doing?"

"Jim. And yes, still married," I offered. I tried to invoke my superior body language skills to convey subconsciously that I was in a hurry and just couldn't stop to chat today. Or any day. Ever. Just go away. Shoot, did I just say that? No, Carolynn was still smiling and talking. All I could hear though was the droning of bees again rather than words.

Just nod. Smile. Agree. Repeat.

My body language attempt had failed. Sigh.

"So are you working now?" I smiled and asked, forcing feigned interest. I tilted my head to the side. That looked more like I cared, didn't it? That was a nice touch. I mentally patted my back.

"Me? Of course not! You DO know I'm a member of the Green Hills Country Club, right? I'm just forever busy attending lunches and banquets, I just don't know how I would squeeze in a job too! AND I'm on the PTA, so that takes up a lot of my precious time too! Are you still doing that teacher thing? Is that volunteer work? I do love volunteer work!" Carolynn chirped.

"No, they pay me. It's a job. Certainly keeps me busy! Oh and speaking of busy, I —"

"Oh you must find it so rewarding to work with children! Changing the world, my friend Liz! Greg and I think teachers are just so important. He's away this week on business. His firm is doing so well, they just keep sending him all over meeting up with clients! I keep busy, and good thing I've our Nanny to help with Elyse! She's such an energetic 7 year old! Sara is SUCH a help though!" Carolynn went on.

"Yes, I would imagine that DOES make things easier for you! Oh, it has just been SO wonderful catching up today!" I told her in an attempt to end it all.

"Oh most definitely! Let's meet for lunch one of these days! You MUST call me!" Carolynn said as she reached for my not-quick-enough-hands for a squeeze. Could she feel them sweating?

"Absolutely! Any time!" I lied.

Oh no, here it was again, another unsolicited hug. Get off. Get off. Get off. Her tiny arms gathered me in, held tight. A few seconds too long, even by my standards. I suddenly realized maybe Carolynn needed this hug. I gave in. My arms returned her squeeze this time.

"Now, don't you be a stranger! We just have so much in common, I'm sure we could talk for hours!" said my dear "friend".

And with that, Carolynn scurried away down the center aisle to get all the things she didn't need. She would take them back to her immaculate house in the best part of town. Lawn greener than the hills of Ireland in the front. Pool sparkling blue in the back.

I went to the self-checkout, otherwise known as the quickest exit lest I see her again. As I pushed my credit card into the reader I glanced to my right and saw a familiar looking man in a red baseball hat. He was scanning a box of...hmmm, interesting. And two packs of gum. A young woman walked up to him nonchalantly looking at her phone and the two walked away together. So. That must be Sara.

    I took my detergent, but I wasn't thinking about MY dirty laundry as I walked out of the store.

MIDTERM EXAM

Don't panic. Don't panic. As long as the exam questions don't involve the French and Indian War, or anything from like the 1700-1900s, I'm golden.

Well here we go...

Name: Jennifer Carver *(Do we get points for our name? I hope so, and it seems fair to give points here.)*

Please read the questions carefully and answer completely for full credit.

Question 1: Evaluate the extent to which the Seven Years' War (French and Indian War, 1754–1763) marked a turning point in American relations with Great Britain. Further analyze what changed and what stayed the same from the period before the war to the period after it. Cite specific examples from the course readings, as well as additional sources you have utilized throughout the course.

Funny you should ask this, Professor Davies. You see, while this episode in history is probably extremely important, the episodes of Ted Lasso were far more pivotal this semester, in my opinion. I'm sure the Seven Years' War established a lot of things. Like, really great things no doubt. The French and the Indians probably had a hearty handshake following that fight. LIke after the soccer matches in the show. And that war, it's like when Rebecca gets a divorce in Ted Lasso, and things are rotten, but then she's able to cope with things. I'm sure that's how things worked out for both sides of that war. Because a divorce can be like a war, right? Am I right? Two sides that can't seem to find a solution. Then the lawyers get involved. Then there are all those fees. Like in a war. Like! In the Seven Years' War! I'm not sure the total dollar amount in damages. It very well could have been in the article you gave us to read (that I really did intend to read eventually), "Implications of the Seven Years' War". And if I had to wager a guess, it was probably on page 3, because page 1 and 2 were likely backstory information before the real meat of the article. That's generally how these articles run. Right? But we all know that nobody actually really reads them all the way. A good skim is a good skim, Professor.

So now to address what stayed the same and what changed, before and after the war. Well, I'd have to say that people never really change. Take my ex, Paul. He said he was at the library studying, but do you know where he really was? Studying Rachel Sanders in her dorm room. Of course I believed him when he said he was studying, but then when Melissa told me she saw them going to a party and leaving from Rachel's, I confronted the traitor. Wars are full of traitors, and the French and Indian War likely had traitors just as despicable as Paul. And that war lasted seven years. I'm fortunate my relationship with Paul didn't last that long. I wasted long enough on him. But you know what? I do miss him. Those were three very intense weeks that we dated, Professor Davies. It's like even when things end, are they really over? Like, did the French people and the Indian people just go back to the way things were? You can't just forget when someone wrongs you. Maybe the French accidentally keyed the Indian's cars in the middle of the night because they had a few drinks and it made them feel better. Maybe the French threw eggs at the Indian's apartment door. Are these war crimes, or means for a restraining order? I think not.

Question 2: In a well-developed essay, discuss the importance of Jonathan Swift's "A Modest Proposal", published in 1729, as it related to the economic state of Ireland.

Jonathan Swift was way out of line with this entire thing.

I mean, even if conditions were bad in Ireland, the solution is not to eat children and sell them. Yeah, I guess it would reduce the number of Catholics in Ireland and stimulate the economy and help with food shortages and all, but I'm really not sure if it's ethical. I'm a vegetarian, so if I were living in Ireland I would not even eat chicken let alone children. What would all the vegetarians in Ireland in the 1700s do if this were their only option? When I became a vegetarian it was because I love animals so much and couldn't eat them. I also love children, so I would not have been able to eat them either. Paul was not a vegetarian but I was ok with that because I was so in love with him. I wonder if Rachel is a vegetarian or if she eats meat like Paul. He probably broke up with me because I'm a vegetarian and don't think he should have ten-cent wings on Fridays at the bar. Those were innocent chickens who lost their wings and can no longer fly because he enjoys them in a sweet and spicy sauce appetizer. But in the sense of economics, as with Ireland, maybe it makes sense. Maybe not everyone can afford to eat fresh fruit and vegetables all the time. I think Ireland also had some potato issues, so there's that too. Paul loved mashed potatoes. He may even have been Irish. If he didn't break up with me like literally right before exams I would have had more time to look things over, Professor Davies. But Paul doesn't care if he ruins my life. Paul only cares about Rachel and her short leather skirts.

Question 3: What was the Indian Removal Act of 1830? In a well developed essay, explain how it affected Native Americans. How did the Trail of Tears have an impact on the Cherokee and other Native Americans?

The Indian Removal Act was an underhanded and dirty way to get rid of people that were once very important to America and then BAM! Just send them on their way as if they weren't already planning Thanksgiving Dinner with their families, complete with matching shirts. And we all know the Indians were very important for Thanksgiving Dinner. So maybe now Paul will be having Thanksgiving Dinner with Rachel instead. But will I cry a Trail of Tears about it? Will I lay awake at night texting and posting my poems about him on Instagram? Maybe. Does it impact him like things impacted the Cherokee and other Native Americans? Why isn't Paul crying a Trail of Tears over me? He told me I was the first girl who really "got him" and appreciated him the way he should be. But do we know a good thing when we have it or are we quick to just "relocate" people for other people. Know who should be crying a trail of tears? It's Paul. Because he will be sorry he lost me. Just like America was sorry they lost the Native Americans. And then they tried to get them back. They didn't call campus security every time one showed up unexpectedly. But everything will be just fine. My therapist said everything will be just fine! Maybe the Native Americans have closure now after everything that transpired. And I'll have closure just. Like. Them.

Click here to Submit Answers. Grades will be posted three days after the last scheduled exam date. Best of luck!

TEACHER OF THE YEAR

Here's a little secret. I have no idea what I'm doing. How is it they don't know? After all these years?

I placed my travel mug of hot coffee (and only a little Bailey's) on my desk and checked the time. It was 7:45am. I had fifteen minutes until my class of adoring students filed in, took their seats, and performed whatever tasks I found on the pages of the yellowed lesson plan from the closet.

I took a sip of coffee and opened my school email. Trainings, new sign in procedure, nothing exciting. I noticed an email from my principal directly to me, not to "faculty" like all the others.

Keith,
We finally filled the 9th grade English position, and he starts tomorrow. You are being assigned as his mentor. No better man for the job than the Teacher of the Year, in my opinion. Please touch base with him tomorrow morning. He's a little green since he just graduated, and never having taught before, he's a little nervous. Most importantly, he's Joe Potsko's nephew so we need to send a warm welcome and help where we can. You know what I mean.
Gary

Wait, what? Mentor? A fresh out of college nephew of the school board president? No. This couldn't be. Did I mention I have no idea what I'm doing?

Here's how I've operated since I was accidentally hired ten years ago:

Go to work. Drink coffee. Assign a page from the antiquated lesson plan book found in the closet. Drink coffee.

Collect (but do not read) assignments. Give the kids I like an A, give the kids I don't like arbitrary Bs and Cs, choose one F for good measure to serve as an "example" to the others. Done.

Somehow this merited Teacher of the Year status on more than one occasion. I still don't know how that happened.

Oh, back to how I was accidentally hired. Funny story. I was trying to get into the school gym to shoot some hoops since my gym membership expired. Security stopped me cold, told me only authorized personnel would be permitted inside. I bit my tongue, though I wanted to let fire a few choice words. I mean, I pay school taxes! Isn't that pretty much the same thing as a gym membership for the school gym?

As I walked away, I saw a suited man approach security and tell him he was there for his interview. Without even a second thought, he was let inside and to his own devices.

I walked off and hatched an idea. I'd show up the next day wearing a suit over my gym clothes. Tell security I was there for an interview, then once inside sneak over to the gym and lose the suit.

The next day, I did just that. Security bought my story, let me in, and I headed for the gym.

My path was blocked by an anxiety ridden woman clutching a clipboard and directing me to the main office for my interview. I barely had time to respond as she clutched my elbow and half dragged me into the principal's office. I had flashbacks of my teen years where the same thing happened just about weekly.

I figured I'd go through the motions because how long could it take? Then I'd get to the gym and unwind.

Well, a perfect storm of my charm and their desperation lead to yours truly being offered a position effective immediately. And I didn't really have much else going on since I was in between jobs (enjoying unemployment) so I accepted and started the next day. Figured I could sit in a classroom and babysit during the day, then shoot hoops at dismissal because a school schedule is pretty sweet. Did I mention I have no idea what I'm doing?

So. Now I need to mentor this kid, with all the knowledge I found in the classroom closet in a box marked "Mr. G's English Lesson Plans - 1988." Why reinvent the wheel? I just followed what he wrote and somehow that earned me Teacher of the Year status on more than one occasion. Papers on the "The Pearl", an autobiography assignment that took up three weeks, sprinklings of grammar tests...it was gold! I found out from some ancient coworkers that Mr. G was a school legend, and passed away recently. In a way, I was paying tribute by using all of his well-thought out work. Or so I tell myself.

***

I walked into the 9th grade hallway the next morning, made my way to the new kid's classroom and found him standing terrified at his desk. The look on his face and sweat on his forehead screamed "walk all over me". I rolled my eyes and introduced myself.

"Pleasure to meet you sir," the kid squeaked as he shook my hand with what felt like a wet trout of an appendage.

"Pleasure's mine, kid. Listen. You'll do just fine. Any questions before the herd crashes in?" I asked.

"Um, actually yes, actually, I..."

"Great! Ok! See you at lunch then! Good luck, kid!" I said and parted the sea of incoming freshmen, ready to feast on the fresh meat cowering in front of them. I did my part. I "touched base", now it was up to him to hit a home run.

***

I decided to check on my mentee at lunch. I had heard the whispers and hallway talk about the "new teacher", and it wasn't good. First period convinced him it wasn't actually English class, but Breakfast and he was supposed to take them all to the cafeteria. Which he did. After the entire class grabbed trays of waffles and fruit cups, the cafeteria worker remarked how kind he was to buy his class breakfast on the first day. His teacher account would be billed. Strike one.

After that, he was wiser second period. No trips to the caf, but his Honors English class had him believing they weren't issued grades due to their past history of outstanding academic achievement. Attendance was optional, as well. And eight students excused themselves to sit in woodshop instead. Strike two.

Period three went a little better. The class stayed in the room, but they didn't stop talking and walking around the room long enough for any amount of teaching to occur. Someone had written on the whiteboard "Mr. Dork" instead of "Mr. Dorn", and that somehow went unnoticed in the chaos of the 42 minute class period. Strike three.

"Out to lunch?" I asked as I walked in and saw him gathering his things and packing his bag.

"Out for good. I'm done. Leaving. This is not for me. It's been awful!" he said as a tear formed in his defeated eye.

I grabbed his bag and dumped it out in front of him. He gasped as his shiny new Teacher Planner and ballpoint pens danced across the fake wood of his desktop.

"No deal, kid. You aren't leaving yet. Not today, not tomorrow, and we'll see about next week. Eat lunch, steel yourself, and know you can do this. They're just kids. They'll see what they can get away with, but if you squash that right here and now, they'll relax."

"But I don't know how to squash anything! I don't even squash bugs!" he said, as he slid his glasses firmly up his nose.

"Straighten that awful tie, eat your PB and J you undoubtedly brought for lunch, and try again. Nobody here had a great first day. Teachers are giant balls of nerves whether it's Day 1 of your first year, or Day 1 of your fortieth year. You got this, kid."

As I walked away and left him shaking with his fruit snacks, I knew he'd be ok. Getting past the first day would give him courage for the next, and so forth til summer break. And against my better judgment, I'd see to it that he stuck it out til then. Note to self: search closet for "Mr. G's Mentor Box" today. Can't hurt to check.

THE GUIDE

Gerald gripped the side rail in the entranceway of the museum, turning his knuckles white and palms red. His tie was too tight, his shoes too big, and his socks rather sweaty. They were probably gaining more strength in stench the longer he shuffled his awkward feet near the guest desk.

It was opening hour on a Tuesday, so the crowd was rather light so far. He watched as an older couple entered, followed by a group of smartly dressed women who were holding arms with each other and chatting as if it's been years since they've gone out.

"You've got this," he told himself as he watched them make their way to purchase tickets. He closed his eyes. It was almost VanGogh time.

Gerald had dreamed of working in the art museum since he visited with his fifth grade class on a field trip years ago. The other children rolled their eyes and huffed in disappointment when they found out where their End of the Year Big Trip was headed. Paulie and James had been sure they were going to the amusement park like the fifth grade had done the year before. They had visions of roller coasters and bumper cars, cotton candy and ice cream. But apparently, the school board decided it was not "educational", and tabled it for a trip to the art museum instead. Gerald hid his excitement when it was announced, and feigned disappointment for the sake of his social status. Then, he remembered he had no social status, and smiled.

Gerald straightened the name badge clipped to his pocket, and straightened himself as the small crowd grew larger. He thought they resembled a bunch of grapes in a still life, their heads an array of sizes in the fruity pale green cluster. The cluster was inching closer, his tie was feeling tighter, and he willed himself to release his sweaty red palms from the slippery silver rail.

Stepping forward, he smiled and folded his hands in front of him. He felt he looked very official, wearing his suit and even carrying a clipboard and Bic pen. He tapped the pen nervously against the top of it, and pretended to count the number of patrons awaiting their guided tour of the art museum.

Once it appeared he had everyone's attention, he cleared his throat and began to speak nervously above the dull hum of their conversations.

"Hello, good morning, welcome!" he said with a squeak in his voice.

The crowd smiled back at him, and became quiet, awaiting direction from their distinguished tour guide.

"We will begin our tour now, if everyone can please follow me through the doors on your left. Stay close together, and please, no food or drink inside the museum for the safety of the precious works of art you are about to experience," Gerald said, the spirit of the task ahead taking hold and steering his thoughts and words.

Gerald led the group into the first viewing area, which contained a collection of works by Monet and Manet. He explained the use of color, brush stroke, and allowed the group to chat amongst each other their views on the varied canvases. He listened in and offered his opinions as well, surprised at the ease in which he was able to converse with complete strangers. This was all going better than he thought it would. They seemed to be enjoying themselves, and valued his insight on the works.

"While Water Lilies is most likely his most famous work,

others such as Poplars have been very well received too," he told them.

"Let's move around the room and compare and contrast his use of color, and the overall mood it conveys," he ventured further. The crowd complied, intrigued with interacting.

Next, he led them to his favorite area of the museum: VanGogh. He debated saving it for last, but it just didn't make sense to circle back to it. His eye caught Starry Night, and Sunflowers. He felt a tingle rush through him. He gazed at the paintings, and could barely contain his excitement. He turned to his loyal crowd, and began to tell the life story of VanGogh. A man suffering mental illness, gaining fame for his work only after his death. They listened in complete silence, in awe of his knowledge. They looked at the paintings Gerald described, as he guided them through each one. Finally, after learning about each painting, it was time to move on.

Gerald finished the tour, each collection becoming easier and easier to explain. When he left his group in the main entrance, they clapped and shook his hand, thanking him for the experience. They had never known there was so much involved in the paintings and artists, and were walking away with a new appreciation.

Gerald smiled. He had no idea how this would turn out. He'd never guided a tour group before, and felt he did an outstanding job. He set his clipboard and Bic pen down on the desk, and sighed a happy breath. He removed the name badge clipped to his pocket, setting that down on the desk as well. Pretty soon, Frank would be showing up for his afternoon shift and would wonder where his name badge and clipboard had gotten to. Gerald laughed to himself at how easy it was to show up and take a name badge and clipboard from the Employee Sign In table. He'd always wanted to lead a tour at the museum, and today he did it.

As he walked out the door, he thought about serving coffee at Starbucks. He'd always wanted to try that as well. He made a plan to get up bright and early, head to the Starbucks on the corner, and commandeer a green apron. He always had a "new hire" story ready, just in case. But usually nobody asked too many questions. He didn't even have to take a name badge the day he "worked" at Lowe's. Once customers began asking him questions about the best light fixtures, one thing just led to another. Same at the grocery store. Pretty soon, his resume would be full of job experiences, letting his heart be his guide and seeing where the wind would take him.

GHOSTLY CHARACTERIZATIONS

Raising the dead is not an easy job. Just ask Gretchen. She has been tasked with this tricky venture for years. How is it she got so lucky? Well, she sort of just stumbled into it.

Gretchen is a 60-something, introverted, book loving, people loathing, crochet crafting librarian. Every day, she wakes up, drinks her tea, and sets out on foot to the local library where she rules the roost and rafters. She demands silence, respect, and book spines perfectly aligned on the shelves. Soldiers in the fight against screens, ignorance, and illiteracy.

One day, as she stood at the end of a row eyeing the spines, she saw something (or someone?) move quickly past the other end. Her internal alarms sirened in her head at the disruption of peace in her sanctuary. She quickly moved to cut off the perpetrator, only to come face to face with the wide wondering eyes of a child. But, this child appeared to have drifted straight from the pages of a Laura Ingalls Wilder book in row L, third shelf down, in the Children's Section. A small double braided head of hair turned around and tried to run away, only to stop abruptly in place at Gretchen's authoritative scream-whispered "Halt!"

Gretchen slowly began to realize that she could see through the child's small figure at the shelves of books behind her. Her floral dress and apron smock hung to her shins, with black buttoned boots on her see-through feet.

What was this witchcraft? Was she the victim of someone's optical-illusioned prank? The child could not be real. What was she doing in the library? How did she get here?

"Yes ma'am?" the child said, and brought Gretchen's attention back to her.

"Who are you, child? How did you get here?" Gretchen whispered.

"I'm Laura. Where am I?" the vaporous child asked.

"You're in the library, child. Where...where do you live?"

"I live in Minnesota. Is this Minnesota?"

"No, child, this is Pennsylvania. But you're safe. The library is a safe place," Gretchen tried to reassure.

"How can I get back home?" Laura asked.

"Now that, I'm just not sure of. Yet..." Gretchen replied, trying to think of how it all could have happened.

She thought back to the morning, and if anything unusual had occurred. She notices everything though, nothing could have slipped by her watchful eye. She arrived early and let herself in, locking the door behind her until the posted "Open" hour of 8am. She went to the circulation desk, deposited her purse in the bottom right door, then deposited her lunch of one peanut butter and apple jelly sandwich in the refrigerator. She placed her water bottle on the desk, and began to put away the books that had been returned the previous day. She put away a Grisham, a King, and two Hoovers. (She would not admit to anyone one was hers, but we know it was.) Then she remembered. She also had to put away a Wilder, making her way toward the Children's Section and wondering if she had enough time to open the door by 8. She decided to hold onto the Wilder book, open the door, and then return it to the basement where the Children's Section was located. But she never made it there. A man was waiting to enter, and immediately asked Gretchen to help him find some books on installing bathroom sinks. Home repair was hardly her forté, and of very little interest to her. She knew where the section was in the library, but rarely ventured there. She had set the Wilder book down somewhere as she escorted the man to the correct aisle.

"Come, child. You are going to help me find a book," she instructed the obedient apparition.

"Yes, ma'am," Laura replied, seemingly happy to have an adventure ahead.

The unlikely pair scoured the library from top to bottom, looking everywhere for the book. It was as if the book entirely disappeared with the appearance of Laura. Could that be what happened?

Having completely searched the library, Gretchen began to search her brain again.

"I opened the door, talked to the man about sink repair, and set the book...wait! I know! Follow me, Laura!" Gretchen loudly whispered (it's still a library, no shouting even when excited).

The two went to the alcove area by the main entrance. Within the alcove, there were bulletin boards with yard sales posted, an empty umbrella holder (it had been unusually dry lately), and a small table pushed back against the wall. On the table, a beautiful clay dish had been newly added as the centerpiece. The dish was an earthen brown and dark green swirled throughout. It was glazed with a coating that made it very shiny, especially when the morning light came through the window and landed inside it. It was a donation to the library, left in a box at the door about a week prior. The note simply said "For the library, where characters come to life, and anything can happen within its walls." There was no name included, and Gretchen had simply thrown away the note after reading it. The clay dish was exceptionally beautiful, and she knew she wanted it displayed right at the entrance. And that is where she left the Wilder book when she opened the door. She was absolutely certain of it.

"It's not here," she whispered, staring at the glittery shine of the dish.

"Are you sure that's where you left it?" Laura asked.

"Yes. Most sure. I left the book, then you appeared. Laura, let's do a little experiment. Come with me to the Children's Section. I have an idea."

And the two set off again. Gretchen knew exactly where to go. Once in the basement, she led Laura to the Dahl collection. She squinted at the titles and ran her finger across the glossy edges of the books. She found the one she wanted, threw a smile at Laura, and pulled it from the shelf.

"Got it. Let's go back to the alcove. I have a theory, little one. And if I'm right, well, maybe I'll cross that path when we get to it."

Gretchen and Laura made their way to the alcove, and back to the clay dish. Gretchen took the book she held in her hand, and gently placed it in the dish.

"Now, child, we will leave that there, and get back to work. Come with me. I'll show you the rest of the library. You can read, can't you?" Gretchen asked, wondering if the little girl was ever taught.

"No ma'am. Never learned yet. But my momma and sisters know how."

"Well, looks like I have another job ahead of me."

"Really ma'am? You'll teach me?" Laura asked with excitement.

"Of course! If you're going to be in a library, you'll need to learn!" Gretchen replied, giddy with the thought of being able to open the door of reading to the child.

Just then, a copy of Pride and Prejudice floated from behind them, dropping with a thud onto the circulation desk. Gretchen smiled.

"Is that you, Matilda? Come out where we can see you!"

And a mischievous mousy brown haired girl stepped out from the classics section, grinning from ear to ear.

"Matilda, meet Laura. And I'm Gretchen. You two wait for me in the basement. I'm going to check out that man's books on sink repair, then we have a lot to do together!"

The girls linked ghostly hands, and skipped off toward the basement. Right through the man holding three home repair books, walking towards Gretchen.

"Find what you need?"

"Yep! And if it all goes South, I'll be back for some books on marriage counseling when my wife reminds me she wanted to call a professional!"

Gretchen laughed as she handed over the books, wishing the handy-husband luck in his project. She could hear the sound of laughing from the basement as well. It had been quite awhile since she found herself laughing. It did not come easily for her, as it seemed to come naturally for children.

Gretchen kept her discovery a secret. One by one, she brought to life her favorites, who then roamed the library with her and each other. She taught Anne Frank how to type on the computer, Alice (who always wondered) how to land a Google search, and Max to use Paintbrush to draw his favorite wild things. She came to see screens as something useful as she raised her ghosts, wanting them to experience more. She steered clear of bringing adults to life with the mysterious clay dish, preferring the interactions of knowledge eager urchins from her beloved tales.

And so she continued, spending her days where indeed, anything can happen.

HAUNTING 101

I accidentally died the other day. And do you know what? It didn't come with a manual. Shouldn't there be a manual? I'm used to everything having a "How to...", a YouTube tutorial, "Haunting for Dummies" even. But no. Heart stops, here you are, don't forget your towel.

So far it's been a whirlwind of adjustments. Once I realized I was dead, as I stood by my body, I wasn't sure if I should just hang out for a while there or if I needed to check in somewhere? Again, no manual. Was there a Hotel Death awaiting my check-in with a mint on the pillow?

I had been sick for several days, so urgent care prescribed an antibiotic. I looked forward to feeling better soon, but apparently I had some sort of reaction to it and things went drastically in the other direction. And here I am. Or, am not? In between? I really didn't know.

I decided to wander, so said goodbye to my body and headed outside. Can I walk through doors now? Yes! Well that's pretty neat.

I walked through the door and it appeared life was going on as usual despite my death. Would the news station show up at my door? Would there be an investigation? Could I somehow fulfill that promise of vengeance upon my college roommate I made years ago and frame her for my death?! Oh the possibilities seemed endless!

I was considering how to frame my ex-roommate when an older man rushed right through me. It was the strangest feeling. As he passed through my now lifeless body, a rush of vibrations traveled from head to toe and it seemed that the experiences of his lifetime meshed with mine, and I could sense what he was thinking and feeling. He was late. He was in a hurry, and blamed his dog Barkster because he took too long finding an acceptable spot to do his business this morning. Then his coffee spilled on his briefcase as he was grabbing his bagel, and now he was about to be very late for a very important meeting. I felt bad for the guy. I sensed he was a good man, as I had seen his lifetime play out in my head at rabbit-speed playback when he passed through.

I decided to follow him. Could I possibly do something to help? Maybe have a ghostly intervention on his behalf?

I saw the building he worked in just ahead, and rushed to the large main entry. I saw the man who Robert (my new friend) was supposed to be meeting. This man looked all business, stern face, wrinkles filled with determination and power. He was jabbing repeatedly at the elevator button, no doubt on his way up to the meeting room on the 8th floor where Robert worked. I floated through the closed doors of the elevator. In no time, the elevator had arrived and the doors began to open to let Mr. Bigshot in. I had no idea if I could manipulate things in the living world in my newly found state, but I tried anyway. I closed my eyes and concentrated as I pressed the "doors close" button. To my delight and Mr. Bigshot's dismay, it worked!

"What the...?"

Mr. Bigshot pounded the "Up" button again, the doors began to open, and I pressed the "close" button again. This was highly amusing!

We continued our game until finally Mr. Bigshot got so aggravated, he yelled over to the main desk in the lobby that someone needed to come and fix the elevator before he's late for his meeting.

Meanwhile, I glanced at the doorway and saw Robert assessing the situation. He took off to the stairs, and climbed the 8 floors as if his job depended on it. (It kinda did.)

I continued to close the doors, then decided to just send the elevator up to the 12th floor, and stop at every floor on the way down to give Robert some time to prepare. In the lobby, Mr. Bigshot was on his cell calling Robert's boss to let him know he would be a few minutes late to their meeting.

I floated up the elevator shaft to the 8th floor, found Robert casually sipping a coffee with all his documents in order on the conference room table. Crisis averted.

So, now what?

I decided I liked the idea of helping people out where I could. I went back to the street and walked around some more. I spotted a woman who looked to be about my age, blindly walking down the sidewalk toward a crosswalk and looking around in her purse for something. I made my way over, and she passed through me. I felt the rush of vibrations, but this time something about it felt different. Rather than see the person's past, Deanna was her name, I saw her future. I saw her crossing the very street we were on, and not seeing the car that was about to turn the corner. The driver was checking his phone for a message he had just received, and took his eyes off the road for just a second. But long enough not to see Deanna and hit her. I saw her in the hospital and everyone around her crying. I saw the family leave and the sheet pulled up over her face.

I didn't know what to do. Could I stop this from happening? Could I make her pay attention and give her more time in her life? I felt as if I needed to try.

Quickly as I could, I went into her purse, took out her wallet, and threw it to the ground. She was just about at the corner, ready to cross. I waited to see if she'd notice, if she'd stop long enough to pick it up and let the car go by before it hit her.

"Ugh! How did I drop that?" she said, stopping to pick up her wallet. As she put it back in her purse, she stopped again.

"There it is!" she said as she pulled out a business card for a hair salon and typed the address into her phone.

Just then, the black car that was about to end her life sailed by safely, avoiding contact with anyone or anything.

Deanna crossed the road, having found what she was looking for, and most likely made it to her hair appointment rather than the hospital today.

Is this how guardian angels work? I wasn't quite sure, but I decided it was how I wanted to spend my afterlife. Now, if only

I could find the manual...

DEATH WISH

"It wasn't supposed to be this way..." Becky whispered as she stood next to Connor's hospital bed. Connor's heart monitor beeped in rhythm, as Becky looked at his pale face. Nurses bustled around busily outside the door, and Connor's parents sat in the room with their heads in their hands.

"Why did this happen?" Kathleen asked the air. Dan put his arm around his wife, offering his presence, not answers.

"The doctor thinks he's going to be ok, do you think he will be ok Dan?" Kathleen desperately searched her husband's face for reassurance.   Tears streaked her makeup-less face, her eyes told a tale of sleepless nights.

"Yes, I think he's going to come out of this and be ok. Becky..." Becky glanced over, Dan hung his head.

***

Becky had met Connor in Science class. She was new to the school, having moved from a small town in Illinois to New York. Things were so different. Life was so different. But meeting Connor had made everything right for her.

"Need a seat?" he had asked that first day.

"Actually, yes. Thank you," she nervously replied, and sat next to him at the lab table for two.

Connor was friendly, popular, and the most attractive boy Becky had ever laid her blue eyes on. They hit it off immediately, and pretty soon became inseparable. By Halloween, they had formed a bond Becky had never felt before.

"Are you sure about this?" Becky had asked him, as they sat together on Mark Hufford's basement couch. His annual Halloween party was in full swing, with music blasting and all their friends showing off their costumes. Too old for trick-or-treating, this was the best way to spend Halloween.

Becky and Connor had dressed as Romeo and Juliet. Cliché? Yes, but they both felt it was most fitting for them, and were excited to make their appearance as the famed lovers.

"Definitely." Connor replied, with a kiss to her forehead.

"You guys ready?" Mark asked in a creepy, whispered voice.

"Let's go," Connor replied and hopped off the couch, pulling his Juliet with him.

Connor had explained to Becky that every year, his friends go to Mark's party then at midnight, sneak over to the abandoned brick school building at the end of his street.

"Legend has it, on Halloween, the ghosts of all the kids who went there roam the halls. That school is so haunted. I swear I've seen kids in the windows before, staring out with blank looks on their faces. Kinda like Greg in Algebra!" he'd said, and started laughing.

"Do you really believe in ghosts?" Becky pressed.

"Course I do! And after we go there on Halloween to write our names on the chalkboard, you will too."

"I don't know if I buy it. Guess I'll find out soon enough!"

The group made their way to the abandoned school. The moon lit their way, and the crumbling brick building appeared in the night, looming with a menacing air before them.

"So, you guys never dared to go all the way to the second floor classroom and write your names there?" Becky asked, wanting to verify Connor's story.

"Nah, always get too freaked out and turn heel. But this year will be different. Right guys?" Mark said.

"Exactly. This year will be very different!" Connor laughed.

"Ladies first, Becky. Let's do this thing." Connor said, and took her shaky hand in his.

The rusted lock on the front door hadn't kept anyone out for years. But nobody really cared, or bothered to replace it. Everyone knew the building was spooked, and few dared to go in it.

"Where's the key?" Mark whispered to Connor when Becky had stepped inside.

"My pocket. It's all set."

The two exchanged a knowing look, and continued inside.

"Did you bring a flashlight or anything?" Becky asked, feeling her way through the hallway.

"Nope. Only moonlight to guide us. It's part of the rules." Greg answered.

"The stairway is right in front of you now Becky. Let's go up." Connor instructed.

Once upstairs, the moonlight through the windows clearly illuminated a classroom on the right.

"That's it over there," Mark said, pointing to the doorway.

Becky heard a muffled sound…laughter? Coming from behind her.

She went into the classroom, and tried to see around her. Old wooden desks, chairs, a large teacher's desk in the corner all covered in dust and cobwebs. She looked to the front of the room, as a child would have so many years ago. She saw writing on the blackboard in white chalk. Moving closer to make it out, she saw scrawled "Mark Connor Greg". No sooner had she read the names than she heard the slam of a door, and turn of a key. Laughing wildly from behind the door, Connor yelled, "Now we'll see if you believe in ghosts after you spend the night in there!"

Mark and Greg ran down the hall, and out the front door as fast as they could, as they had planned.

Making sure the door wouldn't open, Connor turned the knob and put the key back in his pocket.

"All it will take to get out is a quick call to your parents. Check your pocket, Connor. I have your phone," Becky calmly said from behind the door.

"How the hell did you get my phone?" Connor screamed, looking for the key again in his pocket.

"I took it as we walked up the stairs."

Connor opened the door, and went inside the classroom to see Becky sitting on top of a desk.

"Alright, joke's over. I'll take my phone back now. Come on."

"Not so fast. Aren't you curious why I would think to take your phone?"

"Actually, yeah. You wanted the flashlight?"

"I wanted to bait you back in here."

"Bait me? What are you talking about?"

"You underestimate me. All this time, did you really think I wouldn't question why the most popular guy in school would be with the overly average new girl in town? It didn't take a genius to figure out your password on your phone. Your football number and birthday. I've been reading your messages this whole time. Just waiting. Planning. You never cared about me. You were going to break it off right after Halloween, after you guys pulled your prank and locked me in overnight."

Becky made her way to the window, and opened it. Below, a large collection of broken cinder blocks, pieces of desks, and other debris made for a rough landing for Connor's phone.

"Becky, no, you don't understand. It was just a joke. All of it. Dating you, the haunted school…we were just going to have a laugh. You get it, right? No hard feelings?" Connor pleaded.

"No hard feelings? Are you serious? You made me believe we were in love. You talked about going to the same college, a future together!"

"Listen, just give me my phone, and we can go back to Mark's and talk it all over. Just get your arm back inside the window."

"Oh, are you worried I'll accidentally drop it? Well, accidents happen you know…"

Connor was done negotiating. He sprang forward and grabbed Becky's arm. The two struggled in the window, before the wooden frame gave way cracking in all directions. The pair tumbled down, into the heap of debris below.

**

Becky watched as Connor slowly opened his eyes, then squeezed them shut again to block out the bright light above his bed.

She ran her nails down the length of his arm, drawing thin

lines of blood.

If he made it out alive and she didn't, she planned to make him live to regret manipulating her the way he did.

She tugged his IV line, and a series of beeps alerted the nurses who came rushing in.

"He's pulled out his IV, he's awake!" they excitedly told his parents.

Leaping to their feet, Dan and Kathleen rushed over.

"Connnor! You're ok!" Kathleen said as she took his hand.

Becky knew he'd never really be ok. Hell hath no fury, and her haunting would know no bounds.

Connor opened his eyes, and a chill coursed throughout his whole body. He sensed something, or someone, near him. He could feel a sort of negative energy by his side. He couldn't quite be sure, he was so very groggy, but he thought he heard a soft whisper. It sounded like…no, it couldn't be. He heard it again. "Actions have consequences, Romeo…"

Connor jerked and looked wildly around the room.

"Easy, easy. I'll get him something to relax him. All of a sudden his heart rate skyrocketed and he looks like he's seen a ghost," the nurse said.

Connor gripped the side of the bed. Becky stood back and smiled.

UNCOVERED

Victoria

Mary Beth Keegan was about to stumble upon the most monumental story of her fledgling journalistic career. How did I know? Because I was the one planting it right in the palm of her naive little hand.

I met Mary Beth in my History of the English Language seminar class, three months ago. She stumbled through the doorway of Davis Hall, nearly dropping her Old English Dictionary on her flip-flopped foot. She took a seat at the long discussion table, far away from my intimidating podium of dark walnut.

I raised a brow, yet smiled at her, not wanting to frighten the already skittish mouse who appeared ready to cry or run at any moment. I folded my hands on top of the podium, waiting and watching.

As the others made their way in, I gathered the course syllabus to hand out because I've always been old school in my approach. Yes, everything was accessible online, but I still kept to my tradition of handing out the syllabus on the first day, making expectations known, and having each student sign/tear off/turn in the last page. It was a statement of academic integrity, each student vowing to uphold the utmost standard of behavior. Was it legally binding? Not at all. Did it help to let them know I was not just a pretty face and pushover? Absolutely.

The small group of 8 students was an ideal size to discuss the origin and evolution of language. Small group was what I liked best. More intimate. I could get to know the students better, dissect their personalities, categorize their characters. It was how I came to know Mary Beth, and her position as school reporter for The Stygian Speaker, our school newspaper.

To say I'd been plotting and planning could be a stretch, but when the opportunity presented itself, I grabbed hold and moved forward in my objective.

Mary Beth was the key to everything coming together. Or, should I say, coming apart for a certain Head of English Department, Eric Graves.

Dr. Graves was jealous of me from the start. The faculty adored me, the students requested me, and I was keen on taking his position in the upcoming years. And he knew it.

He had played a part in the interview process, and never let me forget that it was his go-ahead that secured my appointment to the department.

Once hired, he requested private meetings far too frequently for my liking, making up excuses to review curriculum or other nonsense. When the meetings were scheduled in the evening, he often asked to order-in dinner. Then he insisted on going out to dinner, because "it would only make sense to grab something together." I agreed, not wanting to offend. I knew how to play the game.

One night, alone in his dimly lit office, as I perused a possible Classical Literature Anthology, Graves inched closer. I could feel his warm bourbon breath on my face as he leaned in, feigning interest in the book. He took a sip of his drink, then set down his glass. His hand found its way to my lower back, then lower. He stood over me, bending down to whisper "I think you know why I've been scheduling these meetings, Victoria."

"Clearly you value my opinion and knowledge of what we need in the department, and know you aren't capable of important decision making yourself?" I replied as I stood up to face him.

"Is that what you think? That's so cute, no really, simply adorable," he laughed.

When he put his hands around my waist and pulled me to his mouth, I pushed him back against his bookcase of collectible classics.

"I believe that's all, Dr. Graves. I will let you handle the decisions now, and see my way out," I said as I slammed his office door. I could hear the sound of books being thrown against it as I made my way down the staircase to the front door of the empty building.

After that, Graves did everything he could to give me the most difficult classes to teach, horrible time slots to offer them, and refused requests for Teaching Assistants to help with the endless grading of exams and papers.

Until Mary Beth.

When I requested the young mouse to help in my overwhelming responsibilities, Graves seemed quite interested.

"So you can't handle your responsibilities and need a little helper? I always knew you lacked what it takes to be any good at your job. Why I recommended your hire is beyond me. Yes, Victoria, you may appoint a helper to do your work," Graves said with a sneer.

"That's *Dr. Fields*, if you don't mind. And I'll submit the paperwork in the morning for you to sign off."

As we parted ways, we glared with venom glistening in our eyes at each other. Our dislike for each other stemmed from different places, but it manifested in our daily interactions all the same.

But soon, I would be the one smiling.

"All done with that stack?" I asked Mary Beth.

"Yes, all done and ready to start the next ones!" she replied, sliding her glasses back in place on her little pixie nose.

"You are amazing. I hope you realize that. And I appreciate you so much. It certainly makes life easier when you feel your worth, right? Though, I can't speak for that much around here," I dramatically offered, gazing out the window with a frown. I needed to be convincing.

"Oh, why would you think that, Dr. Fields? Everyone here respects and admires you so much!" Mary Beth argued, taking the bait.

"Well, you see, not everyone feels that way. And it's not my place but…oh nevermind. Would you like a cup of tea while we work? Earl Grey?"

I made my way to my electric kettle and plunked two tea bags in oversized mugs.

"Dr. Fields, you can trust me. And sometimes getting things off your chest can help you feel better about the situation," Mary Beth offered with a concerned look on her face.

"I know I can trust you, it's just, if Dr. Graves ever found out I slipped his secrets he would…oh I've said too much already!" and I clasped my hand to my mouth to sell it.

"Dr. Graves? The head of the department?"

"Yes. Maybe you're right, maybe if I only told you, I would feel better about the whole thing."

We took our tea and sat at the little table by my office window. I stared into my mug, then locked eyes with Mary Beth.

"He isn't what he seems," I whispered. Mary Beth leaned in closer, her hands wrapped tightly around her mug, waiting for me to go on.

"He told me in confidence that he's been taking bribes from students for years now. Everything from exam grades to scholarships within the department. He wanted me to be a part of it, but you know me, I could never do something underhanded. I told him I refused to take part in his schemes, and he has made me regret it since. I could report it, but who would believe me? I haven't worked here as long as him, and I don't hold his clout. If only there were a way to expose him…but, I suppose we will just have to accept it. Wrong as it is."

"What if there IS a way? What if we expose his story and let them investigate? They're bound to find the evidence!"

I held back my smile, and reeled in my catch.

"Do you think? Can we possibly find a way? If it's of any help, I believe he keeps a folder on his bookshelf with dollar amounts, initials of names, that kind of thing. It's next to his rare edition of Othello. That would provide proof if someone were looking." I offered.

"Leave it to me, Dr. Fields. I know just how to take care of this."

I knew she would run this story in the next edition of the

paper. Someone would find the file I planted while in his office working late with him. Then it would be a matter of time before his time ran out. I couldn't have found a better puppet than Mary Beth, barely needing to pull the strings to make her do my work.

I sipped my tea as Mary Beth hurried from my office, undoubtedly poised to write her article.

Mary Beth

"English Professor Accused of Taking Bribes Fired From University" by Mary Beth Keegan.

It was the expose I'd always dreamed of, uncovering a scandal and becoming a hero to my peers.

"Cheers, to a fine job!" my delighted professor said, as we clinked a celebratory glass of champagne.

"You know, we never liked each other. You really did the entire University a favor."

I smiled as I sat on Dr. Grave's lap.

"I would do anything for you, you know that," I said as I downed my glass.

"She really underestimated you, giving you the exact proof to leave in her office after you published the story about her taking bribes from students. Brilliant, my darling."

"I knew it was just a matter of time once you assigned me to her, before she gave me something to work with. She didn't see it coming, and seems she greatly misjudged where my loyalty falls."

"Yes, you certainly know when you're being manipulated, don't you," Dr Graves said as he stroked my hair.

In my lap, I pretended to check a text message as I leaned back into Dr. Graves chest. I opened my recording app and pressed the button, then set it nonchalantly on my leg. He was focused on his glass of bourbon.

"Tell me more, Dr., about the way you hire new professors here. I can't believe you've been doing it for so long, and nobody has found out!"

"Well, sometimes you just know how to get around red tape, and convince the right people. Let me tell you how I got Dr. Richards his position..."

"Yes, I can't wait to hear," I said as I moved my phone closer on my lap.

DIARY DEAREST

Diary Dearest,
Today is my birthday. And YOU are my present. I asked for a Barbie with different outfits to change up but I guess you will do. Nobody talks to me here or even at school so now I can tell YOU EVERYTHING! And you can't say go away or call me Smelly Kelly or push me into the basketball pole on the playground. I asked Daddy for chocolate cake for my birthday but he said no. He says no to everything. He's just the worst. AND he's drinking again. I hate when he drinks because his face gets extra red and angry. I bet he doesn't even know I turned 9 today.

Diary Dearest,
I made a friend today. She's a new girl at school. Her name is Maria and she's so nice to me! She's so pretty too. Her hair is brown and curly and I wish my hair was curly too. She is super smart and can read any book in the library if she wanted to but mostly she likes books about horses. I told her I have a horse and it's white so it looks like a unicorn and her name is Daffodil. I told her I can ride Daffodil any time I want and my brother can't because he's too mean. Like Daddy. They both don't get to ride Daffodil but if I had a mom I bet she would be sweet as pumpkin pie and I would let her ride Daffodil. She would teach me how to braid hair and we could braid Daffodils tail.

Diary Dearest,
I sat with Maria again at lunch today and you will never believe what she did! She put a brownie on Jackie's seat right before she sat down when nobody was looking and so it looked like Jackie made a huge mess in her pants and then EVERYONE was laughing and Jackie was crying and it was hilarious!! Nobody saw her do it except me and I didn't tell on her even when Mrs.

Shultz got crazy angry and told the class we HAD to tell her who did it. Zip it lock it put it in your pocket. That's what I told Maria and then we laughed and laughed! I'm so glad Maria is my friend. She looks out for me. But I can't ask her to come over. I don't want her to meet Daddy. He smashed up the TV last night and then got angry that I didn't clean it up fast enough. Charlie just stayed in his room and pretended he didn't hear it.

Diary Dearest,
Me and Maria had fun again at school today. You know how our coat rack is right by the bathrooms in the hall? Well Maria thought it would be funny if we took Danny's lunch box after recess and really quick went into the bathroom and dunked it in the toilet then put it back. At lunch he couldn't even eat anything in his lunchbox because it smelled like toilets and was so gross! Danny tripped me in gym class yesterday and I hit my elbow so hard I cried and the other kids thought it was funny. But Maria didn't laugh. She just looked at Danny and I KNEW she was hatching a plan. Sometimes I wonder if Maria was kicked out of her last school. She sure can get her paybacks to kids. But I don't care. She's my friend.

Diary Dearest,
Maria keeps asking to come over. I keep saying no but she may just follow me home one of these days. And then what if she asks Charlie about Daffodil and he's all like who is Daffodil. She has to stay away. And maybe Daddy will be drunk too. No. She can't come here. I hope she's not mad at me.

Diary Dearest,
Well just like I knew, Maria followed me home anyway. She said she didn't care what my house looked like or if Daddy was home, she'd hide and he wouldn't see her anyway. So I said fine. But if he comes out swearing and hitting just run, like I do. She said she would and I believed her. And she did! Daddy was being rotten, Charlie was locked up in his room again ignoring it all, and then

Maria left to go home and I got in bed to write and go to sleep. Goodnight!

Diary Dearest,
Maria came home with me again today. She said she doesn't mind how Daddy is, she has a plan anyway. So I wondered what her plan was, but she wouldn't tell me. Daddy was passed out on the couch when we got home. Charlie wasn't around. Then Maria went into the kitchen and got one of the big knives from the drawer. She was smiling and then all of a sudden she just cut up Daddy's throat and cut cut cut and there was red everywhere just like Daddy's face when he drinks too much and gets angry. But Maria was smiling. She took the knife to the sink and washed it real good then asked me to show her where the shed was in the yard. I showed her and she buried the knife under the shed in the back real deep. Said nobody would look there anyway. Then we heard Charlie screaming so Maria said she'd see me in school tomorrow and ran off home and I went inside. Charlie was still screaming and then asked why I was laughing. I didn't even know I was. Then the cops came and Charlie said he got home and found Daddy like that and that when I got home after him I must have been in shock to see Daddy like that. I know Maria won't tell. Because best friends zip it lock it put it in my pocket.

Diary Dearest,
Maria wasn't in school today. Nobody even seemed to notice she was gone but me. Me and Charlie stayed with Aunt Brenda last night. She's really nice to us kids. She said we didn't have to go to school today and Charlie stayed with her but I said why wouldn't I go? But now Maria is gone. It's ok though. I bet Maria will come back...when I need her.

MISSING CAT: REWARD IF FOUND

My head upside down, legs in the air, I listened without interest to the drone of adults talking. I was in my pajamas, laying upside down in one of the white wicker chairs my dad repainted about every three years or so. Sometimes the paint stuck to my sweating legs when I stood up, and I'd meticulously peel the spots of white.

The thermometer on my back porch that summer night read 87F. It hadn't cooled off at all since the afternoon when I was in the pool. The faint smell of chlorine from my towel, thrown carelessly on the back of a chair, mixed with the humid air trapped inside the enclosed back porch. Nightsongs of crickets echoed from the dark outside, while the frantic flights of a variety of bugs zipped around the deck light shining into the backyard.

My neighbors from behind our house, Sam and Dana, had pushed aside the green plastic coated wire fencing that separated our properties to come over. My father had cut it to easily venture back and forth between our houses. No children of their own, I invited myself over quite often to visit them. I was a delightful child, wasn't I? I'm sure they loved my unannounced arrivals. In any case, they always greeted me with smiles and snacks, so of course I went back frequently.

But that night, they came to visit with my parents and enjoy a peaceful summer night chatting with glasses of iced lemonade. The heat made the glasses sweat giant beads of water that collected in little elf-sized swimming pools on the glass top table.

My ears perked up when I heard Sam bring up their neighbors. I knew those neighbor's kids the way only kids know other neighborhood kids. There were the ones you ride your bike with to the next town in secret, and the ones you avoided. These were the ones you avoided.

Always in trouble, their teen son John spent his time stealing from the Convenience store on the corner and spray painting swear words on the elementary school in town. His sister Jackie was no better, and enjoyed teasing all the kids who declined to play with her. I was one of them.

Just the day before, she had knocked on my door and asked if I saw a cat around that was black, white, and fat. I had told her no, I haven't seen any cats, and she went on her way. I expected a comment on my hair, or a laugh at my Rainbow Brite tshirt. But no, she just surprisingly left. I shrugged it off and returned to my Barbies.

Sam was telling my parents how awful those two kids were to each other and also to their pets. Just recently he saw John taking their chubby little furball of a cat and laughing as he made her slide down their old rusty slide in the backyard. He said he came outside and told him to knock it off, that he could hurt her that way. But John just laughed. He also saw him wrap a belt around the cat's neck like a leash, and the poor thing hissed and meowed til Sam stepped in that time too.

Sam's face had turned crimson as he talked about it. Dana put her hand on his arm, an effort to calm him.

"They don't deserve to have animals," he said with anger that had turned to sadness.

I stayed very quiet as the adults talked. I didn't know if I should tell them John and Jackie's cat was now missing.

As I looked at Sam, and replayed his words in my head about some people not deserving animals, I wondered…could Sam have taken their cat away from them?

I hadn't been over to visit in a few days, so if they did have a cat roaming around their house I wouldn't have known it.

I looked carefully at Sam, then at Dana. Did they exchange a knowing glance? There was a cat unaccounted for, one that deserved a better home and life than what it had been given. They were such kind people, the kind you never forget when they are in your life. Could they have taken her?

And I know my father agreed with them. I saw the cans of cat food he left under the bush by our deck. Their cat was an outdoor cat, always wandering and seemingly looking for food. My father thought he was sneaky about it, but of course I knew.

Could my father be involved too? Or on his own?

I had so many thoughts racing around my mind, that I barely heard the scratching at the metal door. My father set down his drink, and got up from his chair. We all sat up straight to see what was going on.

My father opened the door, and in walked a much thinner black and white cat. And in her mouth, a tiny gray fuzzball of a kitten, mewing repeatedly.

"Oh my goodness! Hannah, go get a blanket and towels!" my mother said excitedly.

I ran to the linen closet and brought back an assortment for the mama cat and her baby. She set the kitten down in the blanket, and almost immediately the kitten stopped its mews and nestled itself into the warm softness of the blanket.

"So that explains it," I said with a smile.

"Explains what, sweetheart?" Dana asked.

"Jackie came by yesterday looking for her cat. She said she hadn't seen her in awhile and asked if I had," I told them. They all stared at me, then back at the cat.

"What did you tell her?" My mother asked.

"I said I haven't seen any cats around," I told her.

"But this explains why she was so chubby and not around. She was a little busy having this kitten!" my father explained.

And at that, the cat started meowing and scratching at the door again.

"Should we let her go?" I asked.

"Yes. Let's see what she does," my mother suggested.

My father opened the thin metal door with the window on top, watching as the cat ran off. We sat looking at the tiny gray kitten, when another scratch at the door caught our attention. She was back, this time with a tiny black ball of meowing fur. She set him down in the blanket, and was off again.

Six kittens in total. Each more adorable and fuzzy and precious than the next. I had suspected Sam was behind the missing cat, even my father. But it turns out she disappeared to have her kittens, then brought them to the safest place she could think of to protect them.

We fed her, and she fed her babies, until eventually we found loving homes for each one. Sam and Dana kept the first kitten that arrived, the gray one, and named her Belle. They bought her a little yellow collar to wear.

We opened the door to let the mama cat out many times, but she refused to leave. She was happy, well-fed, and very loved. So of course she wanted to stay.

What about Jackie?

Well, Jackie stopped her bike in front of my house eventually and stared into the large bay window we had in front. And at the black and white cat sunning herself in it.

"Your cat looks an awful lot like MY cat you know. Where'd you get her?" she asked, never taking her eyes off the window.

I nervously looked up from the sidewalk chalk masterpiece I had been creating.

"Oh, you mean Whitney? Nah, she doesn't look like yours. And we didn't 'get' her. She got us," I said quietly, going back to my drawing as nonchalantly as I could pretend to be.

Jackie looked back at me. We locked eyes, and Jackie gave me a little nod.

"She looks...happy," Jackie said, looking back at the window and Whitney, who rolled over and yawned. We looked at each other one last time. Then Jackie peddled away without another word.

I'll never forget my first pet, and the night she trusted us with her life and her babies.

PINDER

"Stop breathing on me," Kerry said through gritted teeth.

"Technically, I'm not breathing. I'm filtering. But I suppose it means the same thing here," Broggo said in reply.

"Ok, then stop FILTERING on me!" Kerry snapped and got up from the couch in a huff.

"I sense displeasure. And I believe it has been caused by me. Am I correct?" Broggo queried.

"Yes, it most definitely has been caused by you! Ugh! How YOU were matched with ME is...is...well it's unexplainable!" Kerry yelled from across the room of her tiny apartment.

"Of course it's explainable. You see, my kind were all entered into the Pinder database detailing our traits. All of your kind were also entered into the database, and through a series of precise calculations and analysis of data we were matched with each other. It is the most sensible way to account for the influx of population of my kind from Sliggo to Earth. We need shelter, and your kind can help us transition to life here. It's quite genius." Broggo explained.

"I KNOW the rationale behind it, you slimy, four-eyed, tentacled creature. I just don't agree with it!" Kerry lamented.

"Article 8, Section 12 of the Planetary Habitation Agreement signed by your President indicates that failure to comply with Pinder placements will result in fines, imprisonment, and loss of citizenship," Broggo reminded Kerry.

"That seems better right now than this living arrangement!" Kerry said, grabbing her car keys and heading for the door.

"I'm going to class. Do not touch anything. Or break anything. Or explore. I'll be home in two hours and will make dinner. Do NOT go near the stove again when I'm gone! I still can't get the left burners to work and I need another fire extinguisher after your last attempt!" Kerry said and stormed out the door.

"I believe we are making progress in our interspecies relationship," Broggo said, turning his blue mouth upwards into a smile.

Kerry slammed her car door, and turned the key in the ignition. It has been over two months since the sky turned an unnatural shade of green, and spacecrafts made of unearthly metals emanating purple lights descended upon Earth. The majority landed all across the United States, with a handful in Europe and Asia. It was uncertain whether more would be coming, but something had to be done. In an unprecedented meeting of world leaders, it was decided that the best way to handle the situation was to welcome the alien creatures, assigning Earthmates to each one. A system was developed and quickly put into place, systematically matching Sliggon and human. Once assigned their Earthmate, they would be able to acclimate to life on this planet in peace. This planet did not need any more help destroying itself, and just maybe the Sliggons could help in an intergalactic partnership.

But some partnerships were a bit strained at the moment. Despite the scientific basis of Pinder, maybe not all matches were, well, well-matched.

Kerry sat in class taking notes on the profound works of various physicists. She couldn't concentrate, and nothing she wrote made sense upon review. She sighed, set down her chewed up yellow number 2, and rested her head in her hands. She had a headache thinking of what Broggo was likely ruining back at home.

Back at home, Broggo was ruining Kerry's favorite dresses as he attempted to color code them in her closet. He did not agree with the current haphazard arrangement, which unsettled his thought patterns. As he pulled each dress down, he tore several and slimed up the others. Tide Stain Remover was no match for whatever chemical composition coated Broggo's exterior.

In an unsuccessful attempt to rehang the clothes, he accidentally tore down the bar in the closet they hung on. He stared with all four of his eyes at the wooden bar his tentacled arms were wrapped around.

"Well. This is not going as I had planned," Broggo said to the spider plant hanging in the window. He always waited for a reply. He never got one.

Kerry closed her notebook, gathered her things, and steeled herself against the thought of heading home to Broggo.

She thought about his attempt to cook her dinner. He took a cup of strawberry yogurt from the fridge, put it in a pot on the stove, and added Cheerios, three Oreos, and several scoops of corn starch. The plastic yogurt cup melted, everything caught on fire, and her kitchen hasn't smelled the same since. But he wanted to make her happy. That's more than most people in her life these days. Maybe she wasn't giving him a chance. She wasn't the easiest to live with either. She was messy, unorganized, and a free spirit when it came to chore completion. She had a motto of "why do today what can be done tomorrow?"

Kerry suddenly swiped right into the drive-thru of Dunkin Donuts. She ordered half a dozen assorted donuts, a chocolate frozen coffee, and a vanilla latte. Even Sliggons would appreciate that, right?

She drove home sipping her latte, ready to present her peace offering. She had lost her temper for no reason, and it wasn't the first time. Maybe being Earthmates wouldn't be so bad after all if she gave Broggo a chance. And nobody (no creature?) could be worse than her last human one. She still hadn't forgiven her for stealing her boyfriend right under her nose, then parading him around the apartment. After living in an awkward, uncomfortable sea of tension for two weeks, they both found a new place together. What was she even thinking? Humans can be awful creatures.

Kerry laughed and thought "Hmph, good riddance to both

of them! Broggo may very well burn the place down, but he's never going to backstab."

And with that, Kerry unlocked the door and went back to her (their) apartment. She watched with a smile as a thankful Broggo inserted three Boston Cremes into his stomach opening.

Maybe Pinder got it right after all.

LILY

I followed Lily to the couch, and gently sat next to her. I could feel the warmth of her small body. Sense her shallow breathing. I breathed her in, wishing I could breathe life and health back to her. I knew not to look at her, and gazed out the window instead. We both knew she didn't have very long, and looking at her thin, frail body only made it harder in our last days together. Hours? We didn't know.

We have been inseparable for years. When we met, we gave each other the briefest of once-overs before connecting. We couldn't have been more different, looking at us. Like her name, Lily was white. And I'm dark as night. Appearance meant little to us. That first day together was so long ago, yet so ingrained in my memory. Since then, our friendship has grown deeper than the roots of the oak tree I was now focusing on in the front yard. A squirrel ran around its trunk, scampering about amongst the fallen acorns. Another season has passed, the leaves would be falling soon, followed by the cold of winter snow. We weathered it all together.

Lily was wild. And I loved that about her. She was an independent spirit, who looked for adventure and trouble. My opposite. I admired the way she didn't care what anyone thought, didn't care what anyone said. When she got mad, she was a destructive force. I didn't dare get in her way. There was a fire in her. Once, she smashed a glass vase full of roses onto the kitchen floor. She stared at her mess, walked away unfazed, and let the water slowly spread between petals and pieces of glass. I wondered if she always had others clean up life's messes.

When we were younger, she ran away. I wasn't surprised, really. When one door closed, and another opened, Lily was sure to take it. She was gone for several months that time. When she came back, I wondered if she would be changed in some way. If being out on her own had made her more mature, more calm. But no, not my Lily. Still wild, loving, and my best friend. She had a tiny scar over her left eye, and I often wondered how she got it. Was it a fight? An accident? It's always been a mystery. Like her, and her past, which I also didn't know much about. But sometimes these things don't matter. Where we come from does not have to dictate where we go. What matters is who we go with.

There was a time in her past I did know, though, and very well. The time she spent battling drug addiction. She would bound into a room, eyes wildly dancing, unable to sit still. I could smell it on her, and knew what she had been getting into. She knew I never judged her, never thought less of her, and that's what she needed at the time. It was daily for a stretch, then she was able to manage with just every other day. It was a slow cutting back, sometimes reverting to daily though when temptation overcame her. But in the end, she was able to make it through a day, a week, a month, then more without needing the high. She replaced it with other things like bird watching. I encouraged that in her, even began to enjoy it myself when we would spend time together. Any time with her was magical. She was the one soul that completed me, made me feel alive, made me see the blue in the sky and the green in the grass. The world was sprinkled with glitter when she was near. I was content. I was me, when I was with her.

But now she was on borrowed time. She was hiding her illness, not wanting anything done for her in what was her inevitable end. I saw her stop eating as much when we would have dinner. A few bites, a bit of water, and she was done. She became thinner, and moved more slowly. I moved slowly with her. The light that was once in her eyes was fading. But not the light in her soul. It made my chest hurt to see her like this. It made me sad, and angry, and I felt like I was underwater trying to breathe but unable to get air. But I kept all this to myself. It was my silent pain, my solitary confinement of feelings. I knew she didn't want pity, or sadness, so I tried to look at it like her next adventure. Her adventure to whatever awaits when we leave here. I knew I would never find another friend like her. She was uniquely Lily. She would always have half my heart as her own. There would never be another to fill that space. I knew that.

I leaned my head closer, into hers. She leaned back against me, and we sat for what felt like ages and seconds at the same time. I loved her soft warmth, the way she smelled. I thought about how much fuller my life had been with her in it. I thought about how lucky I was to have had that in my life, when I knew not everyone has been as fortunate.

And then she was gone.

She left the world as she lived in it, on her own terms. She wouldn't have wanted it any other way, I knew that about her. I was still looking out the window, and a bird landed on the sill, looking in on us, as we had looked out on it so often. He flew away, and I thought maybe Lily was flying away too, up to the heavens. The breaking in me paused for a moment as I thought of Lily being free from pain now.

Now. I would have to go on without her. I couldn't help but think about my own end, when would it come? How would it come? It didn't help to dwell on such uncertainties.

I put my paw on hers, and licked her head, one last time in goodbye.

THE MAILBOX

She had the backbone of an earthworm. Skin as thick as a green grape on a hot summer's day. They said "Be ready for rejection" and "Learn to accept the silence" after a submission. Well, she tried. But she sought validation like a parking garage attendant seeking the time stamp on those little tickets. From her parents, her friends, even her cat Sophocles, who learned to purr the sadness out of her while snuggling on her lap.

How many times would she write rot before her big break? Would it ever come? Oh, she also had the patience of a toddler on Christmas Eve, waiting with fierce anticipation of the shiny gifts to come. Only, hers never came.

She sat at her computer staring at the screen.
Words.
    Words.
        Blah.
            Words.

Another pitiful page in the making. She sighed audibly and woke a sleeping Sophocles, softly purring on her lap.

"All of these stories, and what do I do with them?" she queried the cat.

"Just keep writing them. Someday, one will be good!" she answered herself.

Over the years, she submitted to publishers and entered countless contests only to fall short each time. A mountain of printed rejects filled her dining room. Mount Unworthy, as she came to call it. Did other writers have mountains too? What did *they* do with all the stories?

She had started printing two copies of each story. One to add to Mount Unworthy, and one to deliver at midnight to the mailbox on Sycamore Ave.

She came across the black mailbox with cardinal stickers

on it late one afternoon several years ago. The bright red birds caught her attention, followed by the small blue house behind it with the peeling paint. She slowed her car and took in the rocking chairs (two of them) on the front porch, and rows of marigolds planted neatly in the flower beds. Gold and orange like little flames shooting out of the dirt. Her grandmother had loved marigolds, and always planted them in her flower bed. She, in turn, loved to pop their flowery heads off and pull the petals out, throwing them in the air like bursts of fireworks.

She wondered who lived at 88 Sycamore Ave, then decided she didn't really want to know. She would rather leave it a mystery. And then she hatched her idea of leaving her Unworthies with the cardinals in the mailbox at 88 Sycamore. The cardinals would carry them off. Yes. That's what she would do.

She decided it best (and most dramatic) to make her deliveries at midnight. Nobody in the quiet neighborhood would even notice her blue Toyota Camry idle a moment at the box before its stealthy disappearance in the dark.

The first midnight drop went smoothly. She took her story, "The Lighthouse", to the box, opened it quickly and quietly, made her deposit, then drove away. An owl hooted his approval. Crickets chirped a cheer. She nodded into the night air, her task complete.

It felt cathartic to release her stories to the cardinals. She imagined them gripping the pages with their sharp little beaks and flying steadfast to a land far away. Perhaps a castle, where an imprisoned princess waited impatiently for their arrival. Her only entertainment in a lonely world where she was kept away from people and amusement of any kind.

She never put her name on her work. Only her initials at the end, signed in calligraphied script.

AW

With each mailbox deposit, the weight of repeated rejection lifted to a more tolerable level. Her stories, once released, could turn into anything.

She thought to herself that the worst feeling was knowing nobody would ever read what she wrote. Nobody would smile at her silly similes, or alight at her alliteration. She wished her stories could get out there, even if it made ONE person happy.

But all she had were rejections, and the cardinals on the mailbox.

**

Another story was sitting in the mailbox, and George was excited to get his arthritic hands on it. He balanced on his cane, opened the box, and looked across the way at Mr. Loftus pulling weeds.

"Afternoon, Mr. Loftus! Beautiful day today, eh?" he shouted.

"Beautiful day indeed!" Mr. Loftus returned.

George hadn't always greeted Mr. Loftus when he saw him outside. Most of the time, he just grumbled and furled his brow, before limping back into his house. After George's wife passed away, a perpetual scowl settled into his face. He sat on his porch staring into the distance, eyes glistening, then his head would bow before going back inside. He had placed cardinal stickers on his mailbox, wanting to be reminded of the bird that meant your loved one was still with you. He missed Nancy, and his world was dark and empty when she was gone.

Until one day, a story appeared in his mailbox. It was called "The Lighthouse", a little love story about a man falling head over heels for a woman he met at a lighthouse in Maine. The story made him think of when he and Nancy visited a lighthouse on a beach vacation, only to view it from the ground.

"Climb to the top? Are you mad?" Nancy had squealed when she saw the seemingly endless staircase before her.

"Well, that's how you tour it!" George had said.

"It's beautiful from right here, ground level, no stairs involved." Nancy smiled. George just laughed, gave her a kiss, and they walked the jetty to look for dolphins swimming on the horizon. Such a happy memory.

George didn't know why the story ended up in his mailbox, or who left it there, but he kept it. He liked reading it and thinking of Nancy.

Then, two weeks later, another story appeared. Then another. George began to look forward to visiting his mailbox, always hoping to find another surprise story. He kept them in a pile in his kitchen, and would go back to read them and smile.

"These stories are forming a little mountain now!" he happily thought to himself.

As the stories grew, he began to think about ways to keep them all together easier. He knew Mr. Loftus was some kind of editor before he retired. He decided to check with him about how to get them printed together.

Mr. Loftus took the pile of stories from George, and after reading through them, knew he could help. He reached out to several contacts, and before long, had them printed together in a book. He was so happy to see George excited about something after the death of his wife. He printed the books from his own pocket, and presented George with the final product. "A Collection of Stories" by AW.

George wondered who was leaving the stories in his mailbox, and then decided he really didn't want to know. He would rather leave it a mystery. All he knew for certain, was that the stories made him smile.

BURNING BRIDGES

Jake

The day was cool for June, but Jake didn't mind. The heat of summer could make him laze around all day. She would be home soon, and Jake was counting the minutes. It was effortless to live together, a harmony of coming and going, working and playing. For five years now, it was perfection. At least for Jake.

Something was different now, and he couldn't be sure exactly what. Alicia had been working late, following the moon home and sneaking in the door without a sound. He knew she didn't want to wake him. To see the questions in his eyes. He played along, obedient as always, snuggling close when she finally came to bed. He tried to ignore the smell of alcohol on her as sleep gathered them in and turned one day into the next.

It was Sunday, but Alicia was up and out the door before the dew had a chance to glisten in the sun. Jake woke from a sound sleep, saw Alicia had slipped quietly from bed, and rolled over to stretch. They were supposed to spend the day at the beach. They would sit on the shore on a blanket, watch the waves crash, and splash around in them to cool off. He thought of Alicia playfully splashing him, and was filled with happiness. Maybe she just ran to the store? She'd be back soon. Jake got out of bed and made excuses instead of breakfast.

Hours tugged at his heart, and finally Jake went defeated into the backyard to get some air. He watched the birds, but their songs sounded like laughter. At him. For waiting. He turned to go back inside, as a glint of reflected sun caught his eye. Her car. It was still parked in the driveway. Did she go for a walk? A run? She doesn't do either of those, at least not without Jake for company. Wherever she went, someone else is driving her. Someone else will decide when to bring her home again. His eyes dropped from her car, and a sick feeling filled his stomach.

He slowly made his way back inside.

Alicia

As the sun still lay tucked into the mountains, Alicia had drifted like a ghost onto the floor and across the room. She had looked back at Jake, still sleeping, and a rush of love filled her heart. She folded up thoughts of his upcoming surgery, and tucked them neatly away into the far corners of her mind as she threw on clothes and soundlessly went downstairs. No time for coffee, and the smell was sure to wake Jake. She watched anxiously through the small living room window as a black car slowed to a stop in front of the house. Butterflies.

She eased the door open and slowly guided it closed so the tell-tale slap of her departure would not travel up the stairs to the bedroom and hit Jake.

"Hi!" she said brightly as she got in the car. She left her guilt on the sidewalk as they pulled away. It was going to be a beautiful summer day. She reached over and took John's hand as their eyes locked. She smiled as the sun finally pulled itself up to climb the mountains on the horizon.

Jake

When you're waiting all alone, your mind is free to travel. The past 6 months, Jake had tried to pretend his pain was normal. An ache here, a sharp stab there. But he was never good at hiding things from Alicia. She knew something was wrong when he stopped running like he used to, and their evening walks together became slower and labored. He had been fast, limber, in great shape. As that changed, she knew.

"Can't hurt to get checked out, right?" she queried gently. She had touched his face, looked in his eyes, and tried to convince herself as she said "It's probably nothing."

The doctor had referred him to a specialist, who deals with the kind of cancer suspected. The specialist had said surgery would be the only option. At this stage in the diagnosis,

Jake had a good chance it wouldn't spread if they got all of it. Jake and Alicia shared a glance of acceptance, as tears grew in her eyes before trailing down her face. He tried to be strong, moved in closer to her, as they decided on a surgery date. He was getting weaker, and knew something had to give.

Today would have been a last day out to enjoy themselves before the recovery from the surgery would keep him homebound for weeks. The doctors had been upfront and anticipated a painful recoupment. But that wasn't what was weighing heavily on his mind at the moment.

Alicia

Alicia looked at John as she let go of his hand and fixed a strand of her brown hair. He looked at her and smiled.

"Thanks for coming with me today," John said as he leaned in and kissed her. They had spent the day hiking, complete with picnic lunch in the afternoon.

"I should go now. I didn't mean to stay out so long today," Alicia said, and she realized she had said it more as an apology, to Jake. Her mind was on his surgery. Again.

Alicia had agreed to meet John today to get her mind off things, try to calm herself and relax. And she had a hard time saying no when John had mentioned spending Sunday together when they had dinner. She shook the thoughts from her head, and gathered herself and her purse to leave.

"When can I see you again?" John had asked, with an edge of impatience in his voice.

"I'll be in touch. Soon," Alicia knowingly lied. It would be at least two weeks that she had planned to work from home to be with Jake and take care of him after his surgery. She knew she couldn't leave him to see John during that time.

She opened the front door after she heard John's car pull

away behind her. She walked in the house and saw Jake waiting for her. He was sitting casually in the chair and looked up at her immediately. Before he could even get up, she ran to him and apologized as tears streamed down her face. Her tears fell fast, heavy with guilt and fear. Guilt for John. Fear for Jake and his surgery. She held him close and tried to make things right. He was too tired to be mad. Too tired to question her. Too tired to do anything but sit with her in the moment. He wanted every moment.

"I'm sorry. Today should have been about us. I just needed to get out. I lost track of time, and...I just needed to get out. That's all," she said with her head down. She couldn't look at him. He would know she was hiding something. Hiding the fact that she would be out with John again, leaving Jake behind. She loved Jake. Absolutely loved him. And then John came into her life and filled a void she didn't know was there. John was the kind of confident and attractive that made her heart jump right on top of her words that got stuck coming out.

She remembered when she first met him. She was grabbing a coffee and bagel at The Caff Shack before work. She set her bag down with her bagel as she quickly stirred in her cream and sugar. Usually, too much sugar. A glance at her phone made her stir faster as the time ticked closer to being ten minutes late instead of five. She practiced excuses as she headed for the door, and felt a hand on her shoulder as she opened her car door. She turned quickly and tried to understand what the incredibly good looking man holding a bagel bag was saying to her. A bagel bag. A bagel bag!

"I think you forgot your breakfast! Here, wouldn't want you to remember after you left and have to come back."

"Oh! Thank you!" Alicia finally got out. In all her daydreams about meeting the perfect man, she always had the most clever and witty things to say. And here she was, speechless, trying not to drop her keys and coffee onto her sandaled feet as this man's dark eyes locked on hers.

"Well, have a good day. Are you off to work now?" he said,

smiling.

"Yes, yes I am. I was running late so rushed out without thinking! I'll sometimes stop here and grab breakfast on the way," she managed. Still not dropping her keys and coffee. Good Alicia, she told herself.

"Would it be too forward to ask your name? I'm John. I also grab a coffee here before work. It seems we have a lot in common already," he laughed.

"I'm Alicia. Thanks again for saving my breakfast."

She couldn't believe how silly she sounded. Saving her breakfast? Was it in peril on the coffee station before John rescued it? She could feel her face getting red and she shuffled her coffee to her other hand.

"Nice to meet you Alicia. Here's my card. Let me know if you'd like to get together after work sometime."

He flashed a seductive smile and handed his card to Alicia, who could not believe this was happening.

"Thanks, I'd like that. I'd better run, I'm already late. I'll be in touch!" she said. She watched him walk away and got into her car to process what had just happened. She was an awkward nervous mess and he still gave her his card? She started her car, and pulled away as John walked back to the coffee shop.

When she arrived at work twenty two minutes late, she could not stop thinking about her morning encounter. She was trying to focus on her list of growing emails, but John's card was sitting in her purse beckoning. She took it out and looked it over. How long should she wait to contact him? He had said "sometime", which did not mean today or tomorrow. When did he mean? What exactly is protocol here? It would just be dinner. She didn't have many friends, this would just be someone to go out with once and while. For a change. She told herself more lies as the day slowly slipped by.

She went home and made chicken for her and Jake, forgetting to turn off the oven as she was lost in thoughts of John. Jake watched her absently drift between tasks, and chalked it up to a busy day at work.

The next day, Alicia stole to the seclusion of her car when her lunch break finally came. She palmed John's card and entered the numbers after "cell" on the list of contact choices. Like choosing the correct answer on a multiple choice test: which should she use?

A: Cell
B: Email
C: Office
D: Fax

But she changed her mind and didn't tap the glowing green circle to send the call. Instead, she opened her email on her phone and tapped the pencil icon to create a new message.

"Hi John, I'm stopping for a bite after work today at Luigi's before I head home. If you don't have plans and would like to join me, I should be there around 6. Otherwise, maybe another time. Have a great day! - Alicia" ...and send.

Ok, that was fine, she thought. It was casual, not pleading, and left the door open to join or not join without needing a firm "yes" or "no" from him since she was just going anyway (according to her). Much easier than calling and awkwardly asking. Brief, confident, and open.

At 5:30, Alicia sat at a table for 2 trying to appear casually unexcited. With every sound of the door opening, she shifted to see if John was making his way to her. He did not respond to her email. Maybe he didn't get it. Or maybe he did and was busy, caught up with work. Or maybe he did, and ignored it. Did he possibly forget who she was? She didn't say it was the girl he met at the coffee shop. Alicia's palms were itchy with sweat and doubt. She sipped her drink and closed her eyes. "This is...this is just silly," she told herself, standing up with resolve as firm as dandelion fluff. She grabbed her purse and allowed herself a last hopeful look at the door.

John

Writing a proposal due in just hours, John rubbed his eyes with the back of his hand. He needed to get this out, but he couldn't concentrate. He could only think about the way Alicia's dark hair danced on her perfectly petite shoulders. The way she glanced down and sideways every time she got nervous. The color of her nailpolish (pink) as she held tightly to her coffee cup, whitening her fingertips and ovaling the paper holder.

He quickly read what he wrote and was about to submit to his boss for the final approval, when an email pinged his speakers and a "new mail" icon floated down from the top of his computer screen. From her. An email. He laughed to himself as he read the subject line, imagining her nervously typing to avoid having to call. Even a text would seem too personal to her at this point.

After reading it, John leaned back in his chair and thought about what to write back. And he opted to write nothing. He'd let her wait to see his next move. As he considered his tactic, his phone chimed with a text. His wife.

Alicia

As quickly as she rose, she froze. Her hand was fixed to her purse, her eyes fixed to the man standing in the doorway. John. His eyes met hers and they exchanged a smile. He made his way to her table, never breaking gaze.

"Hey you!" she said with a smile, and immediately felt a squeeze in her gut. That was her greeting for Jake. No, she wouldn't think of that. Of him. She focused on setting down her purse as they both sat down.

"Were you leaving?" he asked.

"No, I just...no! I'm glad you could make it!" she said.

"I have to say, it certainly was a very nice surprise to get your email. I had a deadline today, so wasn't sure I'd make it." he said as he casually took a menu.

"The deadline, dinner, or both?" she laughed.

"Definitely both!" he said as he slid his phone into his pocket. He still had not replied to Megan, his wife. She wanted him to stop for fresh parsley on the way home from work. His lie was ready before he even closed out the message. Pressure at work, blah...

"Have you been here before? Any recommendations?" Alicia quizzed.

"No, I've not tried this place," he lied. It was so easy.

Jake

Another late night working meant another night listlessly walking around the house, before finding his favorite spot on the couch. Today was a good day. The pain meds were helping, and moving around became much easier without the fiery stabbing all around his inside. Jake was feeling hopeful. Maybe they could go on a trip somewhere. Like they used to do. Just hop in the car, and drive without a plan. His surgery was hanging over then like a storm cloud about to burst. They could go before that rained down on their lives. Knowing the umbrella may not help. May not stop the inevitable.

The sun was disappearing behind the trees, and clouds floated by lazily without any sense of urgency as to where they were going. Same as Alicia lately. No sense of urgency to get home. To have dinner. To talk about her day. Maybe things were just busy at work. But she'd always made the time before.

A knock at the door. Alicia wouldn't knock unless she forgot her key. No, even then, the spare is under the grinning "Welcome" frog statue on the front porch. Alicia insisted on getting it last summer when they were walking by a yard sale in town. The croak of the door opening jolted Jake back from his memory of the frog, and he realized it was Alicia's mom on the other side of it.

Christine pushed the door gently, and a quick "Hello?" as she replaced the key to its home under the frog.

"Jake! Hi! Gosh it's been so long!" Alicia's mother chirped.

It *has* been quite awhile. The last time Christine was over, it was St. Patrick's Day. She stopped over wearing her bright green shirt that said "Kiss Me I'm Italian" that she thought was the most clever thing. Alicia and Jake exchanged amused glances, but she waited until her mother left to fall back on the couch laughing (drink in hand).

"Oh, Mother, where does she even get those shirts?" Then she finished her beer and brought the plates that had held corned beef and cabbage to the sink. They did have a nice day.

"Are you hungry? Alicia's *still* not home? That's just not like her! I can't remember the last time she even stayed late at work! I mean, what reason could she have to..." and her words trailed off as she looked at Jake's face, a bubble of doubt popping between them. Jake's eyes darted to the wall to avoid hers.

"Well, I'm just starving. Why don't I get us some dinner?" she softly placated, and Jake agreed.

They ate dinner in silence on the patio, the hanging lantern lights reflecting off the eventually empty plates.

"I should get going home now. I'll text Alicia that I stopped by," she said as she took the plates to the kitchen.

Jake followed her inside, and to the front door to see her out. She gave him a quick hug before disappearing into the darkness. He watched her car pull away, and the darkness and silence crashed into him all at once. He decided not to wait up for her, and let his mind wander and drift off to sleep.

Alicia

As their dinner plates were taken away, and another round of drinks brought to the table and placed down in front of them, Alicia's phone vibrated and the giraffe on her phone case appeared to walk an inch toward the edge of the table. She took a sip of her wine as she checked the message. It was from her mom.

"Hey honey. Stopped over to say hi but you weren't there. Let myself in and ate with Jake. You're right. He's not looking well. Let me know if there's anything I can do to help after his surgery. Hugs."

John was talking, but Alicia didn't hear him. Her mind was on Jake. She checked the time. How was it after 9 already?

"I'm sorry, I just realized what time it is! I really should get home. Thank you so much for meeting me tonight. This was amazing," and her smile showed she meant it.

"Oh, no problem! Yes, I hadn't realized it got so late either!" John said.

They finished their drinks as John gave the waitress the check.

"Keep the change. Thank you!" he grinned at her.

"Are you ready? I'll walk you to your car. It's pretty dark out tonight with all those clouds moving by," he said. He took her gently by the arm as they walked through the door. His touch gave her goosebumps and she smiled. It's been a long time since that's happened.

When they got to her car, Alicia looked through her purse for her keys. Before she could thank him again for dinner, John's hand was under her chin, deftly lifting her face as he softly kissed her lips. She didn't hesitate returning the gesture.

As they slowly pulled back, their eyes met. They smiled.

"See you tomorrow," he whispered, and turned to walk toward his car.

"Tomorrow?" questioned Alicia.

"Coffee. Around 8?"

"Coffee at 8," she returned, as he walked away confidently. She opened her door and sat in her seat, taking in the night. Her stomach fluttered as she replayed John's kiss in her mind, closing her eyes.

As she drove home, she was further from the fantasy of the night and closer to the reality of what was coming. She pulled in the driveway. Hopefully, Jake was asleep. That would make this easier. He's been so weak, and falling asleep earlier and earlier each night.

Alicia crept inside and rather than go upstairs to bed, she sat on the couch and took out her phone. She had saved John's number at dinner.

"Tonight was great. Thanks again! Goodnight."

Send.

John

Dinner went well. Until the mysterious text that appeared

to end it. What's she hiding? Everyone hides something. Secrets are sometimes necessary though, he thought as he took out his phone and started his car.

"Coming home!" he texted his wife. He pulled out into the night.

Jake

She's home. Jake heard the door. She thinks he didn't. A sharp pain pinned him to the bed. He closed his eyes, which pushed a tear from each. He quickly opened them again trying to hide it.

"Hey you," Alicia whispered as she entered the room, seeing Jake's eyes open.

"Here, you're about due for this now," she said as she gave Jake his pain meds. He was thankful she remembered, as he didn't, and took them willingly.

"I love you..."

He drifted off to a restless sleep.

John

John took his ring from his pocket and slipped it back on his finger as he walked into the kitchen.

"Hey babe, sorry I'm so late. There are so many holes in the Jackson proposal and I couldn't leave without some damage control," Jake said as he wrapped his arms around his wife. He did love her. And they've been together for 9 years. Long years that seemed to sand down the edge of excitement for John. She was still beautiful, but familiar. Maybe that was the problem, he thought as she sat down at the kitchen island.

"It's ok, I understand," Megan replied quietly as she gave him a smile.

"It's late, why don't you just get to bed. I'll be up soon. Just going to tie up a few last things here."

"Alright sweetheart. Don't work too hard," she said and gave him a quick hug and kiss before she headed up the stairs.

John's phone buzzed on the table as she disappeared around the landing. He knew without looking that it would be her. Quiet, unassuming, and incredibly good looking. He'd have her in bed before week's end, he congratulated himself with a smirk. Women couldn't say no to him. He knew what to say, how to say it, and how to feign sincerity. Hell, he's had Megan unsuspecting for 9 years as he pursued his "side ventures", as he calls them. Perks of a job that can offer a host of excuses at a moment's notice. He's mastered the art of infidelity, painting his life with beautiful women on a canvas of hotel sheets. On the surface, he's the devoted caring husband all her friends are envious of. She dedicates her Facebook and Instagram to their idyllic life, posting his praises in a social media mirage of perfection.

He checks the message. "Tonight was great. Thanks again! Goodnight."

He considers his reply. Quickly, he types, "Sweet Dreams." Send.

Megan

As she slowly made her way upstairs, Megan heard the telltale buzz echo from the kitchen below. The house was so quiet, how could she not? She sighed. It's the next one. She wondered how long this one would last, and when it started. Not that it mattered much. She's not the first, certainly won't be the last.

She got in bed and debated waiting up for John. The debate didn't last long, and she closed her eyes and turned her back to his side of their cold bed.

Alicia

Crawling into bed soundlessly, Alicia could see Jake clearly in the bright moonlight coming through the window. His chest seemed to be rising and falling rapidly. Too rapidly. Something didn't feel right. She touched him softly. He was burning hot.

"Jake? Jake!" she panicked. He didn't move, or hear her. She gently shook him and his eyes opened to meet hers. Relief.

"We need to get you to a doctor. I'll grab my keys, we can be there in no time. It will be fine."

But she knew it wouldn't.

Jake

The lights were so bright, Jake had to close his eyes to protect his pounding head from the possibility of more pain. He felt the doctor pressing on his stomach, by his legs, getting a feel for what could be going on. He shifted to the right and noticed the IV connected to him. When did they do that? He doesn't remember. Things were a little blurry with the pain. He closed his eyes again.

The door opened and closed softly. He could hear Alicia's voice. Alicia. What had happened? He knew she was slipping away from him. But right now, he was slipping away from her.

"What's going on? What do you think's wrong?" Alicia asked with tears in her eyes and a break in her voice.

"The cancer has spread much faster than anticipated. It's causing a pretty severe shutdown internally at this point. I'm afraid surgery isn't the answer anymore. Not now. He must have been hiding his pain quite well."

Alicia absorbed and processed the words she was hearing, and Jake had silently agreed across the room. He had been hiding all the pain in his life recently.

"What...I mean...how long...what can I do?" she asked to nobody in particular, gazing across the room.

"I would make him comfortable. Enjoy the time you have left. He's getting some strong pain medicine through the IV right now, so as that works into his system he should be comfortable until he's...at peace," the doctor whispered.

"I'd like to take him to..." Alicia's voice broke and she couldn't finish. Tears were welling and flowing. Like ocean waves. That's where she would take him.

"I'll let them know. They'll put together the paperwork

and you can leave. I'm so sorry we can't do more," he comforted.

Alicia looked over at Jake, whose face appeared more relaxed as his pain was subsiding. She steeled herself and walked to him.

"Hey you," she said softly.

Jake opened his deep brown eyes and looked at her with all the love he's felt for the past 5 years.

"Let's go…"

Alicia

They arrived at the beach and made their way slowly to the sand. Alcia had grabbed the blanket she kept in the trunk for spontaneous beach trips like this. There used to be so many. Back before…and she made herself stop thinking of it.

Alicia spread the blanket and they sat together, listening in silence as the waves reached out and caressed the sand before returning back to the great expanse of the Atlantic. She caressed his head, now resting in her lap, in unison with the waves as they gazed into the ocean's unknown.

Jake

Jake stretched up and put his face closer to Alicia's. He could smell her hair and was comforted in the lavender vanilla he had become so used to. Right now, at this moment, he did not feel pain. He thought of how happy they had been the past 5 years. He looked up at her as he rested on her shoulder, life seemingly slipping away with every crashing wave before them. He had no words of comfort for her. There were none that could make this easier anyway. He closed his eyes, nestled in Alicia's arms. He thought back to the first time he saw her. He knew she was the one meant for him in that single moment. Felt it throughout his whole being. He had walked up to her, and she had felt it too. From there, it just unfolded magically and naturally that they would be together. His heart smiled at the memory.

He heard a wave touch the shore, and drift back to sea,

along with his last breath.

***

John

Not wanting her to think he'd been there long, John had only taken a few sips of his now cold coffee. He was certain, without a doubt sure she would have met him this morning. He knows her type. Maybe he needed to up his game? Coffee tossed in the trash, he went to his car and made his way to work. Assume role of diligent worker. He'd played the execs at work to get into the position he's in at his company. Manipulation was second nature to John. He always got what he wanted. What he felt he deserved. And right now, that was Alicia. He would get her. Like the others. And when he got bored, he would move along. Megan waiting faithfully and patiently at home.

Life was pretty great, John thought as he parked his pretty Porche. He took out his phone and pulled up Alicia's number. "Good morning!" Game on, Alicia.

Megan

Mithridatism. The practice of protecting oneself against a poison by gradually self-administering small amounts. Like Mithridates VI, the King of Pontus. And some say Rasputin. John's a poison she can only take in small doses. His late nights "working" were actually a blessing. She could do what she pleased without his condescending comments. When she met him, she had mistaken his arrogance for confidence. Over the years, it's gotten worse. To the point that she can barely stomach an evening of his character. His pompous put-ons and pretentiousness ate at her. And he would never give her the satisfaction of a divorce, a "failure" in the eyes of others. So she found another way out.

Megan chose this house not based on the number of bathrooms or open floor plan on the main floor. She chose it based on the well in the yard. Careful planning and research led her to this well, this house. She had "borrowed" some chemical kits from the school's science lab where she worked. The words "Megan's just a teacher. You know, easy job, summers off, that whole thing. Luckily I have the job that I have, right Megan?" he'd say with a smug laugh. She used the kits to test the water in the well to determine the concentration of chemicals. A coworker had told her in passing once to be careful of which houses you look at because the older ones with wells tend to have contamination. A well-meaning well warning had become her treasure hunt. The treasure? Arsenic. Maybe it wasn't a coincidence that her search for As_4S_4 would take care of that ass.

Her plan would take time, but she committed herself to the course. It's the only thing that made his bravado bearable. Knowing it was working. The infrequent stomach discomfort he complained of would start to get more frequent. Eventually, his internal organs would suffer. And there would be nothing anyone could do. Afterwards, she would call professionals to test her well water after the untimely and mysterious death of her beloved husband. Good thing she only drank bottled water herself, she'd say.

She took the floral container from the shelf that sat next to the sugar and flour. She grabbed his special protein-bran-blueberry muffin and dusted it with a pretty coating of white. Next, she took the powdered sugar and dusted another layer on top.

"These bran muffins would be intolerable without a little sugar on top!" he had once said.

"Yes, intolerable indeed!" she smiled.

Alicia

As the sun began to rise over the horizon, Alicia felt Jake's body become heavier in her arms. She knew he was gone. But she was fixed in the sand. Like quicksand pulling her into darkness. Sucking her heart from her chest and burying it deep in the cold underlayers below the sand's surface. She thought she had prepared herself for this moment. But how can you prepare yourself for this kind of loss?

She was unsure how long she had been sitting there, when she heard her phone. A text. She absently glanced at it, and saw it was from John. "Good morning!" She remembered they were going to meet for coffee at 8. What time was it anyway? Jake was gone. There would be no surgery.

She thought about meeting up with John, and the thought made her even sadder. He wasn't her type. He was a distraction. He was something to think about besides the inevitable loss she was about to face. It was time to think of herself, and focus on trying to find herself again.

With a newfound peace, she held Jake close, buried her face in him, and whispered "Goodbye Jake…I love you…you were the best dog in the world."

THE PROFESSOR'S SECRET

Morning seeped through the window and swirled about the room. Thin white curtains did little to stop it. Bits of dust sparkled in the air as Professor Miles Clark sat with a stack of papers and red pen, reading and grading.

The squeaking sound of sneakers jarred the Professor from his concentration and he turned to look toward the door, glasses slipping an inch down his nose.

"Ah, Julia! Turning in your work I see! It's about time, young lady! You really do like to press a deadline, don't you!" Professor Clark said with a smile.

"Haven't missed a deadline yet, have I?" she replied, passing over her papers.

"No, not a single one! I suppose some of us work best under pressure."

"Is that how you worked when you were in school?" she queried the aging Professor.

"Oh, not me, not me...I'd say I was more methodical. More patient in getting done what had to be done," he said, as that familiar dreamy look crossed his face which meant he was wandering way back in his memories.

Taking a seat in a nearby chair, she waited for the story that was undoubtedly to come.
She enjoyed the Professor's stories, and didn't mind sitting for a listen, despite how busy she knew her morning was.

Professor Clark set down his pen.

"These can wait a moment while I tell you about something, something I've not told anyone," Professor Clark whispered as he leaned in closer.

"Oh? Something that happened while you were in school?" she leaned as well.

"Yes, a long time ago. But it feels like yesterday. Isn't that how memories sometimes are?" he said.

"Quite so, Professor," she nodded.

The Professor leaned back in his chair. He shifted to get more comfortable, and adjusted his glasses. A thoughtful look overtook his face.

"Back when I was in school, things got to be very competitive. In my final year of classes, last semester, I was determined to come out on top. Top of my class, top of my friends, top of the world in my book. I wanted to show everyone who ever doubted me what I was capable of. And in doing so, I learned just what I was capable of to get there," he said as he turned his eyes to the window. A shadow seemed to pass across his face.

Professor Clark's stories were typically about trips he'd taken, books he'd read, or harmless anecdotes. What was he getting at today?

"I never meant to hurt him. It just…happened that way. He was the only student my equal, had been for years. I knew he was the only one standing in my way of being first in my class. First! I had dreamed of being first in my class since the day I started school! I wouldn't let Robert have it. It was mine, you see. I worked and earned it. Robert didn't have to work towards anything. Life was handed to him on a platter, and I was so tired of it. While I spent weekends in the library studying for exams, Robert spent his with his friends. Parties and drinking and drugs, you name it. How did I know? Robert was my roommate. A random pairing by the school, and we became 'friends'. You know what they say Julia, keep your friends close…"

"And your enemies closer?" she finished.

"Exactly. I remained his roommate year after year. Endured, more like. He was intolerable at best. So messy, so loud, so inconsiderate. How was he getting top grades? I knew something wasn't right. I waited. I watched. And I finally got it out of him one night, as he wandered in drunk and blabbering. I asked him just how it was he could party all the time, never study, yet still ace everything. His brain was swimming in booze as he told me how his father made sure he always got the best of everything. Money talks, and the school listened, he had said laughing, then passed out in his bed."

"So, his father was paying off the school to get him top grades in everything? That's just awful, Professor Clark! What did you do once you found out?" she asked.

"Well, I needed to be smart about it. I needed a way to expose him, his father, and the school in such a way as to make them all come clean about it. But my time was limited. It was almost graduation at that point, and I had to act fast. I needed a foolproof plan. And I had one," Professor Clark said and paused. He folded his hands, and looked down at the years gathered in wrinkled hills and valleys across his skin. And then he continued.

"I set him up. I left a note on our door for him to find, telling him to meet at midnight in the alley off Birch Street. The note said 'I know your secret.' Of course he would come, and I had planned to confront him there. I had clothing all in black, even a ski mask and hat. He'd never recognize me, and I'd tell him to come clean about the whole thing or I'd go to the Dean myself. Did I actually plan to do so? I'm not sure. And I never got to find out if I would have gone. Things…went south," he said, his voice trailing off at the end.

"What happened that night?" she asked, her heart racing to know what Professor Clark did to Robert all those years ago.

"I was waiting in the shadows. I had my back pressed to a door in a darkened back entrance to an apartment building. The alley in June stunk with trash as cans lined the small street. I was early. I didn't want Robert to see me coming, so I could surprise him. I saw him coming, right on time. Which was unusual for him, since he was always late to everything. As I watched him make his way down the alley in the dark, a saw a larger dark figure approaching behind him. I nearly shouted for Robert to turn around, to watch out, but it was over before I could even utter a sound. The dark figure swiftly approached, and Robert never saw him coming. He went down to the ground with little more than a gasp. The dark figure went through his pockets, took his wallet, and took off into the night. I stood frozen. I couldn't believe what had just happened. I ran to Robert's body, checked for a pulse, and found none. He was gone. And it was because of me. In a panic, I ran as fast as I could back to my dorm room. I took off my hat and ski mask as I ran, and once in my room, changed out of the rest. It wasn't at all what I had planned. It wasn't at all what I had wanted. And yet...yet now Robert was out of the way. News of the mugging and murder swept the school. Nobody questioned Robert being out by himself at midnight, probably headed to a party they said. Only I knew the real reason he was there that night. In my valedictorian speech at graduation, I was received with a standing ovation. My fellow classmates knew my 'loss', and suddenly I was the most popular and well-liked student on campus. Was I sad about losing my roommate? I'm not so sure. Was I happy about being first in my class? Absolutely. I had gotten what I wanted and worked for. Everything after that fell into place, with acceptance into the best graduate school, and eventually earning my Doctorate and becoming the Head of the English Department. And now, Julia, you know what happened. My little secret is now our little secret, " Professor Clark said with a smile.

"Wow, Professor Clark. That is quite a story. And you've been holding onto that secret all these years. Don't worry, it's safe with me," she assured him.

"I knew I could count on you, Julia, my best student!" Professor Clark replied.

"And now, Professor, I must get back to my work. You know how it is, there's always something to do!" she said as she stood up to leave.

"See you tomorrow with your next assignment!" the Professor called after her as she made her way to the door.

Jen closed the door, and stood for a moment in the hallway. She was running back through Professor Clark's story, and trying to decide if she should tell someone. Would it matter at this point? Maybe it was best to lay it to rest.

She pulled her stethoscope from her lab coat pocket, and draped it back around her neck. She made her way to the Nurse's station, as she did every day after her visit with Professor Clark to "turn in her work", which was a printed Wikipedia article about any classic book she Googled that day. Today she turned in something by Poe, something about a heart. She would give it to the Professor who took out his red pen, and spent the day making notes in the margins and finally assigning it a grade. He didn't have much time left, as the cancer was eating away at his organs. And dementia was eating away at his mind. The doctors had told her his final days in the hospice wing were upon him. She would continue to see him each morning and drop off her work til the end. His best student, Julia, whoever she was.

"And how is the Professor today, Jen?" Kelly asked from behind her clipboard. She was making notes for the morning staff to address at morning meeting before the shifts changed.

"Same as always. Grading his papers, and telling stories. And…I get the feeling he's ready for the end now," Jen said, her face suddenly serious.

"How do you know?" Kelly asked her, seeing the look on her face.

"I think he may have told his last tale…" Jen said, and glanced down the sterile white hallway towards Room 106.

Down the hall, Professor Clark felt a sense of relief having finally shared the truth about Robert. And he closed his eyes.

LOCKED

"Are you kidding me?" Dana thought, as she wrestled with the rusted lock on the oversized metal door.

"Can't they get a new lock? Would that be so terribly difficult?"

Dana crouched down as she jammed the key into the hole. A dim light the color of sulfur struggled to shine above her.

With a click and a clink, she managed to tug the lock open. She pulled it from the chains that wrapped through the door handles, pushing them aside. Her fingers had a light dusting of red orange from the lock, and she thought twice before slipping it in her uniform pocket.

One week here, and already she gets the loathsome job of bringing files to the locked basement in the hospital's hospice wing, the oldest section of the hospital where typically the oldest patients are sent.

She didn't even want to do this ridiculous Candy Striper volunteer nonsense. If it weren't for her mother forcing her to do it, she'd be home sampling whatever trash liquor her father bought that week.

But here she is. Stack of files lodged in her armpit, pink stripes all down her back. Like a pretty little feminine zebra.

Earlier this evening, she was assigned the job of pharmacy runner. That's the only thing making this nightly charade worth it. She goes to the pharmacy window, checks the row of "out" baskets, and delivers the medications to the nursing floors. She checks the labels. She pockets the Xanax and Valium. Not all of it, of course. It's not like they count each pill when it's dropped off. They just assume the pharmacy got it right, and you can't even notice a few missing. A few pills from each, and nobody is the wiser. Seems they should keep better track of these meds, but what does she know, she's just a kid. A sweet looking 15 year old with honey blonde curls, hydrangea blue eyes, and enough charm to fool anyone in her path. Those suckers.

But now the task at hand. Or, in this case, in armpit. She shifts the files to her hands and gets rust prints on the manilla covers. There's a thumbprint covering a patient's name, but she can still read the writing. "Barbara Monroe 1932 - 1994" was printed in black pen on the little tab. Must have passed away this week.

She pulls on the heavy gray door, and it releases a high pitched squeak in protest. The hinges are as rusted as the lock.

Once through the door, Dana can't see a thing. She tries to let the yellowed hall light shine in enough to see a light switch. She takes a step forward and feels something slowly move across her head. With a startled gasp, she grabs at it to tear it away, and inadvertently releases a blast of light from a single bulb above her head. A pull string for the only light she can find. And not a moment too soon, as she was inches from a staircase leading down into a cold darkness. Frigid air hit her face as she moved closer, and her arms filled with goosebumps.

In one pocket, the rusted lock weighed against her leg. In the other, the pills she stole weighed against her mind. She felt for them, decided four would be fine, and swallowed them down. And now down she went.

Her hand found an icy metal railing, and she slowly took the first steps down into the basement where the files were kept. Also kept in the cold basement were rows of recently passed bodies. Because as Dr. Werner had told her, "They won't be looking at the confidential files down there." She politely faked a laugh and sucrose smile at his joke, then took the stack from him to set out on her mission.

In her mind, she counted the steps down.

She was running low on light by step 12, and looked above her for more outdated light sources. Just when she could barely see anymore, the floor evened and the steps stopped. Before her was another door, black this time. Or was it just the dark that made it appear so? Her hands were sweating as she grabbed the doorknob and hoped it would be locked. She held tightly to the files, not wanting to drop them, and gave the knob a slow expectant turn. She thought she heard…no, it was nothing. Was it? She glanced behind her and up the staircase. She waited and listened. Nothing. Just her imagination. Maybe one more pill would help. She swallowed another, opened the door, and stepped into a dark room. She half expected icicles to be hanging from the ceiling as she switched on a light, found easily near the outside of the door.

A row of white sheets covered bodies laid to her right. A row of gray filing cabinets stood to her left. A small buzzing filled the room, escaping from the two bare lightbulbs screwed into the ceiling. One flickered, then went out.

"Great. Next they'll probably have me come down here to change the bulbs." Dana thought as she shuffled her white sneakered feet toward the files.

She squinted in the dim light to try to read the labels on the cabinets, faded from the years. Her eyes focused, and her ears alerted her to a sound in the hallway. A sound of…footsteps? She turned her head and bolted upright, staring at the small window separating life (hers) and death (theirs) in the room, from the hallway outside the door.

"Hello? Is someone there?" she called out.

Silence.

She waited and listened, finally looking back to the cabinets. She was going to file her papers and get out of there. Nobody specifically "told" her to file them alphabetically, so she didn't. She shoved the files in, slammed the cabinet door, and froze.

A hand was on her back.

Then, she was on the floor.

**

Was it minutes or hours later when Dana woke up? She felt groggy, her head was aching, and her right arm was covered in scratches. What the hell happened? She rolled to her side, the buzzing light seemed to buzz louder.

Sitting up, she held her head, and looked at her arm. Were they from an animal? A person? She vaguely recalled hearing something in the hallway. Was it someone looking for her?

She heard a rustling near the bodies prostrate in front of her. The end of a sheet swayed in what seemed to be a breeze, or someone moving past. There was no breeze down here, no windows, no fresh air. Maybe she imagined it?

"Hello? Is someone in here?" she called out to the dank room, voice shaking.

No answer.

Struggling to her feet, she felt her pocket for more pills. They were all gone. Had she taken them all? Had someone else taken them from her? She felt her other pocket. Where was the lock? It was gone. She definitely had put it in her pocket.

She moved as fast as she could to the black door and found it locked. Did it lock by itself once you entered the room? She tried the door again, and began to bang on it.

"Hey! Open the door! I'm down here! Hey!" she shouted at it.

Would anyone come looking for her? Her job tonight was pharmacy runner, so only Dr. Werner knew she had come down to the basement to bring the files. Dr. Werner. He'd come to find her, wouldn't he? She thought back to when he asked her for the "favor." He had glanced around...was he making sure they were alone? Nobody else had heard.

Dana walked back to the filing cabinets. She opened the drawer and pulled out the rust stained folders she had carelessly shoved in earlier. She opened the first one. Empty. Her stomach dropped. She opened the second. Empty. Her heart began to race. She opened the third one. Inside was a single sheet of paper. Typed in the middle of the page were the words "You don't fool me, Dana..."

Dana sank to the floor. What the hell was going on. Her heart was pounding. The last remaining light in the room turned off. Darkness.

***

Dr. Werner slipped the lock into the chains on the oversized gray door. With a clink and a click, he gave a tug making sure it was secure. He placed the rusty lock's only key in his lab coat pocket, smiled, and licked his lips. Mmmm. He had a new "patient" that he was very much looking forward to taking care of. She'll make a great…addition…to his caseload below.

SELF(IE) PORTRAIT

For the third time, Reilly's phone slipped off the table and hit the floor, with a dramatic thud that seemed to say "you failed!" once again. She sighed, picked up the phone, repositioned the selfie circle light attached to it, and checked the timer on the photo setting. Carefully this time, she leaned her phone at an angle she thought would make her face look skinny.

She swiped the mode to "Portrait" setting, and mentally prepared herself for her best smile in 3,2,1.....

Finally! A picture she can work with. She had been setting up her Facespace account for days, and the picture of herself was the final touch.

She had worked meticulously creating her profile. Her hometown was boring, so she filled in a more exciting one several towns over. Her job was nonexistent since she was only 14 and couldn't drive herself to one, but she filled in "Accountant". Why not? Seemed like a cool job. And she was getting good at making a perfect account here, so "accountant" was fitting.

It took two years for Reilly's mom to finally agree to let her have her own Facespace account.

"You're too young! You see everyone you know in school anyway!" she'd tell her. Over and over again. Reilly was tired of the same excuse.

"Mom. ALL of my friends have had their own accounts for YEARS now! I'm THE most uncool kid in school because you're so overprotective!" Reilly had argued back. But, to no avail. The answer was always no.

Reilly's mom told her the Internet was a dangerous place and blah blah blah. Reilly knew how to be safe, not give out personal information to strangers, all the things her teachers have been telling her for years. They even had a program at school about "The Dangers of the Internet", and Officer Richard (who was Gary Richard's dad), came in and presented an entire PowerPoint presentation on the topic. It took up Reilly's whole Algebra class so she felt it was definitely worth it.

When she went home that day, she told her mom about the program, and promised on her dead goldfish Barry's grave that she would be safe online. Still, the answer was always no.

Until now.

Reilly stared at the picture she had just taken. The Portrait mode had blurred the background of her bedroom wall and poster of a kitten with a donut. That was probably a good thing. She made a mental note to get "cool" posters.

The picture still wasn't right. She opened it in another app, PicEnhancer. She set the filter to brighten her skin, darken her eyelashes, and shrink her nose. There. She stared at the new image of herself. Something still seemed off. She saved it, then opened it in another filter a user had created. It was called Moonlight, and gave a darker background, making her face stand out more. The blurred kitten and donut were completely indistinguishable now. Her hair looked lighter against the dark background. Better.

Reilly tapped "save", then saw another filter on the home screen to the app. This one was called Starlet, and made puffy full lips. She adjusted the shade of her lips to a light red, and adjusted the flush of pink on her cheeks. While she was there, she dragged her cheekbones higher. She felt a little giddy with excitement. Her picture was starting to look so amazing! She wondered how many friends would like her picture. And if Nick would comment on it. He said "hey" the other day when they passed in the hall, and Reilly felt her heart begin a gymnastics routine in her chest. She managed a "hey" back, complete with an almost imperceptible head nod of casualness. She was trying to sell the nonchalant acknowledgment of his existence, and in doing so, tripped over nothing just as he rounded the corner. That was a close one.

She was finally ready to upload her picture and activate

her account. She felt a rush of adrenaline as she uploaded her picture into the Profile Picture spot on the page. Done.

Wait.

She scrutinized her picture. No. Not good enough yet.

Her chin looked ginormous in this photo. She went to another app, FaceErase, and shaved off the bottom part of her chin. In lifting her cheekbones earlier, her chin started to look disproportionally bigger. But now it's fixed. Only...only now her right ear seems off. With another swipe over her phone, she minimized the size of her ear. That made her eyes look bigger. And that looked so Disney Princess! She swiped again and made her eyes bigger, and changed the color from her boring grayish blue to bright, almost turquoise blue. Just a little more darkening to her lashes and brows, and there! Perfect!

Reilly hit "replace" on her profile picture and added the new and improved version of herself.

She gazed at her picture, and thought how stunning she looked.

She wrote her first post. Then deleted it. Then rewrote it. Then deleted it. She wanted to sound equally cool and unphased by the whole thing. She wanted to avoid sounding like she JUST started an account, even though she did. She thought of something brilliant.

"Hey new account here, had to. You know, locked out of my other one. Add me here!"

Now people would think she had to start this one because an old one got hacked, and they just didn't know she had one before. Then the "friend spread" would happen. Facespace would start suggesting her page to friends of friends until she grew her list to a respectable size. If she requested friends, they'd see she was just trying to add after being locked out of her old one which was totally cool.

It was starting already! Notifications on her profile picture liking it. Friend requests on her list. And oh! A comment!

Reilly clicked her picture and read the first comment. It was from Amy, in her science class.

"Gorgeous grrrl!"
Reilly smiled. She *felt* gorgeous.
Another comment!
"So pretty!" From Megan, who rides the bus with her.
Reilly decided she could get used to this. She stared again at her picture and grumbled because it was time to go to school. She'd have to keep her phone in her locker til lunchtime, which would be pretty much an eternity.

***

In homeroom, Reilly looked around wondering who saw her new profile picture and account. The first bell rang, and she gathered her books to make her way to English.

"Hey. Saw your new Facespace account," Nick said from somewhere behind her.

Reilly turned and immediately turned four shades of red.

"Oh! Yeah, I uh, had to make a new one. So annoying," Reilly said, kicking at a rock that wasn't there. Obviously, since they were in school. Stop being weird, she told herself.

"Yeah, it looks pretty cool. But, I almost didn't know it was you. I mean, like, the picture and all," Nick said, his eyes narrowing a bit and seeming to look closely at her.

Did he mean he liked her picture? He's talking to her now, so it definitely got his attention. Maybe he realized how beautiful she was after seeing the new picture she created?

"Well, I guess I just wanted to say…you know, the Internet is dangerous, Reilly. You might not like who you see.

"You mean 'what' you see?"

"No. I mean 'who.' See you around," Nick said, as he walked away noticeably shaking his head.

Reilly stood there, as the late bell rang. She didn't go to English, but rather to the bathroom. She stood at the mirror, and looked at her face. At her small eyes. Her big nose. Her short eyelashes and crooked brows. She thought about what everyone else sees when they look at her.

Reilly walked to her locker. She took out her phone, and

saw she had 52 new notifications from Facespace. She opened the app, went right to settings, and deleted the account.

The internet IS dangerous. And maybe not in the way Officer Richard presented.

THE BLACK BOX

Gabby double checked the address in her phone as her small Toyota climbed over rocks and roots down Orchard Road. After confirming she was indeed going in the right direction, she squinted at what appeared to be a massive, ivy covered, red brick building in the distance. The morning sun was cutting through just enough autumn fog to allow her to see it must have been built ages ago. The brick was crumbling, the ivy stretching, the windows coated with dusty memories.

She had received an email giving her a heads-up that a very worthwhile estate sale was taking place Saturday morning. She often received announcements from realtors, and was on several lists to be notified when local sales would be taking place.

Gabby had a keen eye for antiques, and the ones she didn't hang on to, she sold for top dollar. It wasn't so much the money she was interested in, but in being able to earn enough to keep investing in more treasures.

Every old vase held memories of flowers long gone, perhaps given by a doting husband, or an enamored lover. An antique sewing machine hummed its stories of a struggling mother, making clothing for her children in the late night hours after a full days work. Depression glasses were filled with the tears of hungry children, opening the boxes of Quaker Oats to find the free glassware placed inside as an incentive to buy their products. So many stories, so much history. It was the people Gabby had in her heart, their lives and what they had to say. And she wanted to know all of them, all their stories.

She slowly pulled closer to the once majestic home. It surely was a sight when it was cared for and maintained. Now, the grass was overgrown, the flower beds filled with weeds, and the shrubberies threatened to overtake the entrance.

Gabby pulled all the way up in the long driveway adjacent

to the house. She must be the first to arrive, she thought to herself. Which was just how she liked it. Gabby was not a haggler, or one to try to outbid another interested party at estate sales. It just wasn't her nature. She had the mindset that if it was meant to be, it was meant to be. If she was the one meant to take home a piece, then she would.

She closed her car door, and began to approach the front door, an old wooden one with cracked paint and splinters spiking out, daring one to knock.

From the corner of her eye, Gabby thought she saw someone move past a second story window. Likely the person in charge of the sale.

Gabby lifted her hand to knock on the worn door, but it seemed to open before she could make contact. Just as well, she thought, she probably would have ended up with wood in her knuckles.

"Hello? Anyone here?"

Gabby slowly took a step inside, and tried to adjust her gaze to the dimly lit rooms. She looked to her right for a light switch, just as a voice echoed down from the long stairwell in the foyer.

"Good morning, Gabby. Thank you for coming today. I knew you'd be interested in this sale," the voice called out.

Slowly, a figure descended the stairs, almost appearing to float downwards.

"Oh, hello! I received an email about the estate sale today. It seems I'm the first to arrive," Gabby replied to her host. She extended her hand in greeting, and the old woman accepted it with a wrinkled smile.

"The first, and only. I'm Genevieve. I'm taking care of my sister's estate now that she's passed. Helen has a house full of very special, very unique things. Why don't we look around."

"I'm so sorry for your loss, thank you for having me here today."

"No, thank you for coming. Let's get started," Genevieve said and began to make her way into the parlor.

Gabby followed, and gazed upon a room filled with paintings, china, handmade blankets and quilts, and… something caught her attention on an end table.

Gabby walked toward the table, and glanced back at Genevieve.

"May I?" she asked, gesturing to the table.

"Please do."

Gabby picked up an ebony box, crafted of wood, with ornate patterns carved into it. Despite its age, it was far from faded.

"African Blackwood. Open it," Genevieve instructed, as she soundlessly appeared at Gabby's side.

Gabby opened the Black Box, and inside found a mirror on the inside of the lid. The interior of the box was lined with black velvet. She ran her fingers over the smooth material, seamlessly attached.

"This is gorgeous. Such a treasure…is it part of the sale?" Gabby hopefully asked.

"Yes. I was hoping you'd like this piece. It was very special to Helen. I believe you will find it special, as well."

"How much are you asking for it?"

"Not a thing. Only the promise that you keep it, and use it as Helen had. That will become clear soon," Genevieve said, closing the Black Box in Gabby's hands.

"Are you…sure about this? I really don't mind paying you what it's worth," Gabby said, taken aback by the thought of having the Black Box for free.

"It is as Helen would want it. Please, on your way out, stop in the garden where her memorial stone is placed."

"I most certainly will do that. Thank you so much, Genevieve."

Gabby left the house, Black Box in her hands, and saw the memorial Genevieve had told her about. She stopped to read the words written in the stone. "Our Beloved Helen" was clearly visible. But then, something underneath appeared to be written backwards.

"How strange. I wonder what that says..." Gabby whispered, as she traced her fingers over the cold stone. Then she realized something.

"Wait! Maybe if I..."

Gabby opened the Black Box, and used the mirror to read the cryptic writing. She saw in the mirror, "Our last secrets, secret no more."

What could that mean?

As Gabby furrowed her brow in thought at this message, she heard something coming from the box.

Quickly, she looked inside. Rather than the mirrored message, she now saw a face. It was the face of a woman who had a striking resemblance to Genevieve. Could this be, Helen?

"You've discovered the secret of the Black Box, Gabby. It's a very special box indeed. It reveals the last thoughts, the last words, our loved ones wanted to share right before they left the world. To use the box, simply allow the mirror to reflect their picture. They will appear, as I am now, and reveal the last thoughts they have for their loved ones. This box will help with healing after a loved one passes on, and Genevieve and I knew you were the one to have it. She will be gone soon too, and will join me. It's now up to you to help others," Helen said.

"But, why me? Why did you choose me?" Gabby asked, not knowing if she was experiencing reality or a dream of some kind.

"We've known you since you were a child. The mirror has let us see your life, just as you will see the life of the one who should inherit the Black Box next," Helen gently said.

"How will I know who needs my help? Who needs closure?"

"The mirror will show you that too. Once you see who is in the mirror, you will find them and ask for their loved one's picture. Only you will be able to hear their last words. Then you must tell their loved ones," Helen told her.

"But what if they don't believe me? What if they think I'm crazy?"

"Trust me, they won't. This will be what they need, how they can move on. And they will only be thankful to you for giving them that gift. And now, take the Black Box and trust in yourself. Goodbye, Gabby."

And with that, the box closed.

Gabby sat staring at the box in her hands. Did that really just happen? She stood up, and tried to collect her thoughts.

As she went back to her car, she saw a white light start to slip from the carving in the front of the box. Gabby opened the box, and saw an image in the mirror. It was not someone she recognized. Then, as if someone were writing on it, she saw the name "Charlie Gardener" appear below the image.

This must be the first person she needs to find. Gabby closed the box. She started her car, and set out with her new responsibility. One that she felt honored to now possess.

Gabby paused on Orchard Road, typed "Charlie Gardener" into her phone, and found an address. Placing her hand atop the Black Box, she drove to the main road.

It was time.

TOUCHED

Wear clean underwear! That's what they tell you, right? Well, at least your mom does. And why? In case you get in an accident, of course!

Well, I have a little secret. Lean in close...guess what? If you're in an accident, you really don't care what state your underwear is in. Chances are, it will all be a mess anyway. Like the rest of you. I won't get into details, I'll just leave it at that.

The day of my accident, I'm pretty sure I showered that morning. I think. But, it was summer so I very well could have shrugged off the shower before heading outside for a walk.

The afternoon sun was shining, the birds were singing, and somewhere behind me, a car was swerving. Right into me.

I woke up from my coma cloud bleary-eyed, with a tube down my throat in the ICU. (Not thinking of my underwear, mind you.) I couldn't move, but could blink. I blinked at a person standing over me telling me I had a tube in my throat and couldn't talk. Yep, valid. Then they told me I was in the hospital and just rest. They didn't have to tell me twice. How long was I out? A week or so? Long enough. They took the tube from my throat, which felt like I had managed to swallow a garden hose then decided to yak it back up like a hairball-hacking cat. Not a very pleasant experience. 10/10 would not recommend.

Still not able to move, yet I was deemed well enough to earn a roommate in a less touch-and-go setting of the hospital. I bid my private room farewell, and was wheeled whole-bed style to the new unit.

A thin white curtain separated me from my new roomie. Not that I was eager to initiate our first Girl's Night and play Truth or Dare giggling and getting to know her. I could hear her on the phone with someone. She had a thick tobacco accent.

"They said they're going to the house! You gotta lock the

drawer. No! Get everything out you can THEN lock the drawer with what's left...I gotta go. I'm gonna ring for more meds. See ya later." *click*

I tried to think of what needed to be removed and locked up so urgently as a nurse entered the room.

"You need something?" she asked me.

Before I could say anything, Secret Sally barked from behind the curtain, "She don't need nothing! I need meds! The PAIN! It's terrible! Get them now!"

The nurse was unmoved and dryly asked her to please rate her pain on a scale of 1-10. If I were a betting gal, you know I'd put my money on the 10 here. Secret Sally was seemingly desperate. My meds were still being drip-drop-dripped through my IV in a steady flow, "to keep me comfortable" in my broken state. I could only imagine what I looked like based on the gasps and exclamations of horror from the nursing staff when they helped me and saw the bruises that had formed. You'd think they would keep all that to themselves. Like when your kid falls face first into the sidewalk and looks like a crime scene but you tell them it's nothing so they don't freak out.

"It's a TEN! A TEN!" shouted Secret Sally in dramatic wails.

"Ok, I'll be back," the nurse replied, and left the room.

"Hey over there! I need my rest so don't expect me to talk to you. You hear me over there?" she directed at the curtain.

"Yes, that's fine," I managed with my post-intubation accent.

The world was a blur since I had no contacts or glasses (casualty of the accident) to help me see. My vision had failed since third grade when I got glasses, then refused to wear them. I hid them in my desk instead. Since then, I had matured enough to want to see though. But now I could neither see nor feel anything when I tried to move my hands. Sensory input was definitely compromised, but, for how long? Forever?

I clumsily grabbed my phone that was sitting on the bed tray. I held it close to my face, whole handedly, and tried to tap the green text message icon. Nope. It fell from my hands onto my lap in the bed. I managed to pick it up and drop it back on the bed tray with a sigh. Texting was talking and I couldn't do it. I desperately wanted to message everyone I loved, everyone I missed, everyone who felt so far away. And I couldn't.

Secret Sally was on the phone again instructing someone to find a stash of something in the coffee canister in the kitchen. Oh, Secret Sally, that's probably the first place they'll look when they get there, I thought. I wondered how it would all play out. And hoped I wouldn't be in the hospital long enough to find out.

But days stacked up like legos to weeks, and two things happened:

1. Secret Sally was arrested.
2. I was released to a rehab facility.

This happened at 9:30pm, via a one hour dark and bumpy ambulance ride while my wheelchair was precariously strapped into place. My still unworking hands tried their best to steady my neck-braced broken neck for the duration.

I arrived at my new home close to midnight, and was wheeled to the Brain Damaged Unit. Really? Brain damaged? Apparently when you've been in a coma and had head trauma you're labeled as such. If I could feel my hands enough to write, I'd insert "slightly" in front of that. Makes it seem better. Just a bit brain damaged, thank you.

As the staff traded paperwork with my ambulance Uber, I tried to get comfortable in my room before they helped me into the bed. The Velcro holding my neck brace in place had loosened on the ride. Loosened enough for my useless hands to grip it enough and then take off for just a minute of relief from that uncomfortable feeling of being choked 24/7.

Success! I took it off and placed it on the wheely bedside table in front of me. Ah, sweet release felt so good! But, what were those flashes of red lights in the hallway? And why did it appear a SWAT team of nurses were charging full-speed toward my room with terrified looks of concern on their faces?

"Stop! You can't do that! Your neck is broken! You'll be paralyzed!" they shouted.

A nurse nearly dove across the bed to get the brace and quickly choked me with it once again. I thought maybe one would swing in through the window too like you see in movies. No such luck.

They all breathed a collective sigh of relief. Wow, these nurses were dedicated. They pressed the alarm as soon as one noticed what I had done, and immediately sprang into action.

That earned me a place on the unit's "Restricted" list. I wasn't allowed to go anywhere without supervision. I think there may even have been a mug shot behind the nurse's station with my picture and "Mocks Safety!" above it. Look at all I accomplished in only a few hours in Rehab!

The next morning, I opened my eyes, and was immediately met by another pair of eyes and a hand with a large needle that swiftly stabbed my stomach. I screamed. He screamed. My 92 year old brain damaged roommate screamed. Nurses ran into the room.

"Oh my God I'm so sorry! I had to give the daily injection! I thought I could do it while she slept!" nurse Stabby explained. He was clearly new 'round here.

"Did you honestly think I'd sleep through it??" I high-pitch gasped so dogs could probably hear it (if they were also rooming in the Brain Damaged Unit) as I held my throbbing stomach.

"Um, yes?" he whispered, then backed out of the room as the other nurses tried to explain why that was not the best idea.

Wide awake, the nurses got me dressed, washed, and wheeled to therapy. Time to learn to walk again! And, time to train my hands again to feel and move and go back to working like hands. I still couldn't text, hold a brush, brush my teeth, or write my name holding a pen. My fingers felt tingly pins and needly, and I had little strength to do much of anything.

Fast forward: Months of physical therapy finally got me back to walking. Armed with my shiny silver walker and a nice dose of pain meds, I was able to lap Betty around the therapy gym. Betty was my third rotation of roommates, and had a stroke, but she was no match for me. Was I decades younger than her? Yes. But the car that leveled me also leveled the playing field there.

"Hey Betty, you better keep working hard in therapy so I don't smoke you doing laps in the gym again!" I teased her.

"What? Oh sorry, I haven't smoked since '92! My doctor said knock it off unless I want those cancers going around from them!" Betty replied.

"Good for you Betty!" I didn't correct her, and she smiled.

Slowly, I started to make progress feeling again too. Repetitive exercises of squeezing things, moving beads around wires, and all sorts of other ostensibly silly tasks began to help. The numb tingles remained though, even as strength slowly came back. I'd gotten used to the feeling of unfeeling.

I sat in my wheelchair one morning as usual, staring down at my "lucky llama" socks my sister had brought me. We had a theory that socks with llamas could be lucky, and help me walk again and get out of rehab.

"Come on already!" I impatiently chided them.

"I'm sorry, it's your turn now!" a sweet therapist replied.

"Oh! No, I was talking to…" Don't say the llamas on your socks, they already have you in the Brain Damaged Unit, I told myself.

"Nevermind, I'm ready!" I finished instead.

And now, for the amazing part. Are you ready? Out of nowhere, it's as if the Lucky Llamas expanded on their territory and not only lucked my walking, but lucked my hands too.

As the therapist took my hands when I stood, I felt it. Stunned at feeling feeling again, I looked at her wide-eyed and mouth agape.

"Are you ok? Are you in pain?" she panicked.

"No! No not at all! It's the OPPOSITE of pain! I can feel you squeezing my hands! I can feel your fingers wrapped around my hands pressing down! I can feel how warm your hands are!" I rambled as a smile swept up my lips.

"Alyssa! Come here!" she shouted, and my Occupational Therapist dashed over.

"Squeeze my hand!" I challenged her. And she did. And as if her warm squeeze was directly connected to my tear ducts, I started to cry the happiest tears. Then she cried. Then we were all just standing there squeezing and crying. Because it had been the longest road to get there. And because there were so many tears before that, tears not of joy. And then I told Alyssa to grab my phone. I held it and tapped the screen, tapped the green message icon, and watched it open through blurry watered eyes. I made a new group message with everyone on it that was in my heart, typed "I love you", and hit send. My feelings, from finally feeling.

BOOK CLUB QUESTIONS TO PONDER OVER PINOT

1. Did you read the book? (Stop! This is a trick question. Always say "yes", then move on to question 2).

2. Were there any characters that stood out in their morality, or lack thereof?

3. Which story did you feel you connected with the most? Why was it meaningful for you?

4. Which story do you think would make the best movie or series?

5. Were there any quotes or passages that stood out to you?

6. If you could talk to the author, what questions would you ask? (Never math, by the way. Never.)

7. What was your favorite story and why?

8. How many cats are "too many" cats? (Ha! Another trick question! There can never be too many.)

Thank you for reading!

Made in United States
North Haven, CT
18 December 2023